Praise for "The Archaeolojesters" Series

"Kids with a soft spot for Indiana Jones-style adventure will eat up the book ..." – *Movie Entertainment*

"Oertel keeps the tension mounting ... leaving new fans eager for the next installment." – *Booklist*

"... pure fun, succeeds as a fast-paced archaeological adventure ..." – *Kirkus Reviews*

"It is Nancy Drew meets *The Goonies* with a twist ..." – *Children's Literature*

"... a fun, engaging series for adventure and history buffs." – *Quill & Quire*

"... a number of surprising and entertaining twists and turns ... readers will have a ball wondering what can come next." – *CM: Canadian Review of Materials*

"Preteens with a fondness for Indiana Jones will be entertained and educated ... Oertel keeps the action moving while sprinkling the text with fascinating details ..." – *Montreal Review of Books*

BOOK **3**

The ARCHAEOLOJESTERS

TROUBLE AT IMPACT LAKE

Published by Lobster Press™
1620 Sherbrooke Street West, Suites C & D
Montréal, Québec H3H 1C9
Tel. (514) 904-1100 • Fax (514) 904-1101 • www.lobsterpress.com

Publisher: Alison Fripp
Editor: Mahak Jain
Editorial Assistants: Stephanie Campbell, Simon Lewsen, & Ryan Healey
Graphic Design & Production: Tammy Desnoyers
Cover Concept: Elena Blanco Moleón
Production Assistant: Vo Ngoc Yen Vy

Canadian Patrimoine
Heritage canadien

We acknowledge the financial support of the Government of Canada through the Canada Book Fund for our publishing activities.

Library and Archives Canada Cataloguing in Publication

Oertel, Andreas
       Trouble at Impact Lake / Andreas Oertel.

(The archaeolojesters ; 3)
ISBN 978-1-926909-86-8

       I. Title. II. Series: Oertel, Andreas. Archaeolojesters ; 3.

PS8629.E78T76 2011   jC813'.6   C2010-905430-X

Printed and bound in Canada.

MIX
Paper from
responsible sources
FSC® C103113

For Ripper and Jay

– Andreas Oertel

Acknowledgements

I would like to thank Greg and Vincent for enthusiastically volunteering to be my bad guys – even though they're really good guys. Thanks also to Steve Davis, a genuine Air Force brat and a great mentor. And as always, thank you Mahak Jain and everyone at Lobster Press for your continued support.

The ARCHAEOLOJESTERS

BOOK **3**

TROUBLE AT IMPACT LAKE

ANDREAS OERTEL

Lobster Press ™

CHAPTER 1

"I think that's enough," I said.

Eric ignored me, pressed the compressor hose against the valve stem of his front tire, and gave the tube a third blast of air.

PSSSSSS.

"Seriously!" I said.

"I don't know ..." He dropped the hose on the ground and tested the bike tire's firmness by pinching the rubber. The front wheel looked rock hard, and he couldn't even dent it with his fingers. "I'd better fill it a bit more."

"Are you nuts?" I shook my head. "It already looks like it's about to blow."

Eric stopped. "I *have* to put in more air than it needs, to make up for the slow leak in the tire."

"I know *that*," I said, "but it's going to explode if you force any more air in. Remember a few years ago, when that guy overfilled the tire on his boat trailer and it blew up? It killed him and they found bits of rubber all over his body."

Eric stood up and brushed some gravel from his bare knees. "Really?" he asked, staring down at the tire. I had his full attention now.

I laughed. "No, I just made that up. But it could

happen. And then I'd be mad at you for being dead and ruining our day."

"Yeah, okay," Eric agreed. He threaded the tiny cap onto the tire valve to protect it from dirt. "I guess eventually a tire has to blow up. Hey, can you imagine how cool it would be to see a gigantic tire explode? Like ... like from a jumbo jet. Remember how big that plane was?"

I nodded, thinking about the monstrous airliner that had carried us back to Canada.

Only a few days had passed since we returned from our unbelievable trip to Egypt, where we had traveled back in time. But we were already getting bored hanging around town. The community service hours imposed on us for public mischief – from when we fooled the town with our fake plaque – were pretty much served. We had picked up all the litter from all the ditches, and the graveyard had never looked neater. When we finished mowing the cemetery the day before, we decided we had to get out of Sultana for a break, so Eric and I made plans to go to Elbow Lake for a day of fishing.

Eric swung his pack over his shoulder and adjusted the straps. "Did you tell your dad where we're going?" he asked.

"Not yet. As soon as he's done with that customer, I'll go tell him." We were standing beside the service station where my dad worked. Our backpacks were crammed with snacks and our rods were poking out like giant bug antennae – we were all set.

A van towing a trailer had pulled into the gas station at the same time as us. Three people – a lady and two red-haired guys – got out of the vehicle. Dad waved at Eric and me from the pump island, but we didn't bother him because he was busy gassing up their van and the two off-road vehicles (also called quads) sitting on the trailer. The red-haired guys began checking the tie-down straps for the quads. And the lady who had been driving went inside the building with my dad – to pay for the gas, I guess.

"Hey!" One of the guys barked at us. He waved us over to the trailer like it was an order, not a request.

Eric and I pedaled the short distance to the strangers. "Hey," I said back.

"You kids know of a place called Impact Lake?" the taller guy asked. The early morning sun struck his hair from behind so that his head looked like it was on fire. The second stranger – he was shorter and chubbier – wore a baseball cap, but the strands that poked out around the edges were the same color as his tall companion's hair.

"Sure," Eric said. I suspected he was annoyed at how bossy the men were and that's why he didn't say anything else.

I nodded too and looked over the gear piled on the trailer. In addition to the two all-terrain vehicles, I saw bright blue scuba tanks, coolers, and lots of gear bags. These guys were *seriously* prepared for an expedition. The shorter guy was on the far side of the trailer and he kept glancing at the door to the service station. When he saw me roll my bike closer to the equipment, he quickly walked around the trailer and cut me off before I could get close enough for a good look at his stuff. Maybe he thought I was going to steal something.

Big Red sighed. "Okay," he said slowly, "so *where is it*? And *how* do we get there?"

Eric and I had grown used to the many strangers that visited Sultana last month. People came from all over the place to check out the town where a bunch of kids caused a hullabaloo with a phony artifact, even though that steady flow of tourists had trickled since then. Everyone who'd visited had been polite and friendly, nothing like these two divers.

"The turn-off is about nine miles down the highway," I said. "But if you're not watching, you'll drive right past and miss it. The road's not marked. From there you'll have to take the hunting trail – which used to be the old supply road – south for three miles."

The short guy smirked, revealing lots of rotten yellow teeth. "Sounds pretty simple," he said. Then he demonstrated his gross manners by spitting a wad of chewing tobacco on the ground, halfway between the trailer and my bike. *Yuck!* I didn't think anyone used that stuff anymore.

Big Red glared at Tobacco Chewer with a look

that said, *Smarten up*.

Tobacco Chewer looked down at his feet and took a small step backward. Then, after a few seconds, he went back to watching the door of the garage.

Big Red cleared his throat and forced a smile. "So," he said, "once we find the road to Impact Lake, we should be able to find the lake – *and* the abandoned Air Force base?"

"You can't miss the lake if you stay on –"

Eric cut me off. "For twenty bucks we'll show you exactly where the road is."

Big Red chuckled. "I don't think that's necessary, *kid*."

It bugged me the way he said "kid" – probably because he sounded disgusted when he said it.

Eric rolled his bike next to mine, but he stayed well back from the blob of tobacco and saliva on the asphalt. "You guys diving for those sunken planes from the war?"

Tobacco Chewer ignored Eric's question and looked at his wristwatch. "How long will it take to get there?" he demanded.

I admit, asking *what* they were diving for wasn't really any of our business, but it was still a pretty harmless question. "I guess that depends on how you drive, won't it?" I said. "If you hurry, you'll get there fast. And if you crawl along ... well, then obviously it'll take a lot longer. It's pretty basic physics."

"And if *you* stop for breakfast," Eric added, staring

at his beer belly, "it might take all day to get there."

Tobacco Chewer scowled at us and he looked like he was about to say something extra nasty, but the squeak of the service station door behind me inter- rupted him. I didn't turn to see who it was, but the strangers did, and immediately their faces softened and became friendlier.

I looked over my shoulder and saw the lady who had gone in with my dad. She was folding up a map as she walked toward us. She was the same age as the men – about twenty-five – except she was kind of pretty. Her hair was long and dark brown and she had it pulled back in a ponytail – the same way Rachel (that's Eric's twin sister) always did.

She smiled at Eric and me when she got closer. "Hi boys," she said.

Eric and I smiled back. Now *she* seemed normal and nice. *Why couldn't her pals be more like her?* I thought.

"All set?" she asked Big Red.

"Yup," he said.

The men never did answer Eric's question, so I thought I'd try again – this time with the lady present. "So, you guys are going to search for one of those *Harrier* planes that sunk at Impact Lake during World War II?"

Tobacco Chewer ignored me and climbed in the back of the van, but Big Red nodded. "That's right, kid," he said, opening the passenger door.

14

"Wish us luck."

The lady gave us another big smile and said, "Have a great day." She climbed in behind the wheel, started the van, and drove east toward Impact Lake.

Eric and I watched them head out of town on the bridge over the MacFie River.

"That'll be the day when I wish them any luck," Eric said, still staring down the highway. "In fact, I hope they *don't* find those planes."

"Don't worry," I said, "they won't."

"Huh? Why's that?"

"Because there are no *Harrier* planes in Impact Lake."

"Really?" Eric's eyes grew big. "So they lied."

I nodded. "A *Harrier* is a British fighter jet – that's the plane on the poster in my bedroom. And it didn't exist during WWII."

"And it's not a floatplane either," Eric added.

"Right," I said, "the training base at Impact Lake only used floatplanes."

"You'd think those guys would know that." Eric frowned and ran his fingers through his thick blond hair. "Who goes on a diving expedition to recover an airplane without doing some basic research first? Unless they just don't care what kind of plane they find."

"I suppose ..."

"I mean, they look like they know what they're doing," Eric said. "They have lots of gear with them and –"

"But it's all brand-new. The scuba tanks, the dive bags – everything looks way too shiny."

"Maybe they take good care of their equipment," Eric suggested.

"I don't know. In any movie I've ever seen with divers, the scuba tanks are scratched-up, faded, and scuffed – from bumping into stuff all the time, I guess."

"Hmm ..."

"And did you see that guy's wristwatch?" I said. "It looked like it cost five bucks. It's probably not even waterproof."

"Yeah, that's right," Eric said. "My Uncle Oliver dives too and he has a super-cool watch with tons of features. And it has a long rubber strap so that he can wear it over his wet suit. That guy's watch *did* look like a piece of junk."

"On the other hand," I said, "maybe they *just* found out that there's something important or super-valuable – besides a floatplane – at the bottom of the lake. And they quickly bought all that gear so they could get to it before anyone else. That would explain why their stuff looks new *and* why they couldn't answer our airplane question."

"Huh. I'd sure love to know what they're diving for at Impact Lake."

"Me too."

Eric gave the handlebars on his bike a good

spin and we watched the front wheel go round and round. "You know," he said, "I don't feel much like fishing anymore."

I grinned at my friend. "If *you're* thinking what *I'm* thinking, we could be at Impact Lake in two or three hours."

"So?" My dad shouted from the gas station steps. "Have you boys decided where you're going to go fishing?"

Eric and I turned around and pedaled over to him. "Yeah, I think we'll head over to Elbow Lake," I lied. Well, it wasn't a complete lie. Elbow Lake was past the turnoff to Impact Lake, and if we happened to change our minds on the way to Elbow, that didn't make me a liar.

"I wish I could join you boys," my dad said. "It's going to be another scorcher and I'd much rather drop a line in a lake, instead of sitting in a hot garage."

"Did those three people say why they're going to Impact Lake, Mr. Lint?" Eric asked.

Dad nodded. "The young lady's a government researcher and she wanted directions to the old training base. She said she's doing an assessment or evaluation of the base for the government. Something about turning the place into a National Historic Site."

"A what?" Eric asked.

"A Historic Site," Dad repeated. "A giant outdoor museum – you know, like *Lower Fort Garry* or the *Old*

17

Pinawa Dam?"

"That would be great," I said, "having a huge park down the road."

"It sure would, Cody," Dad said distractedly. He was probably imagining all the tourists who would stop for chocolate bars and gas. "But don't get too excited. There's been talk of turning the base into a protected site for years. And nothing ever comes of it."

"Are those other two guys helping her with the evaluation?" Eric asked.

Dad laughed. "I was wondering about that too. But when I asked her if they were her assistants, she rolled her eyes and said they have *nothing* to do with her. They've got their own project, she said."

"Did she say what that project is?" I asked.

Dad shook his head. "No, and I didn't ask. I'm not *that* nosy."

"But isn't access there restricted?" Eric asked. He knew darn well the base was a KEEP OUT zone, so I wasn't sure why he was even bringing it up. "How are they going to get into the area?"

Dad squinted at Eric. I thought he might be getting suspicious and I wished Eric would shut up. "I'm sure they got all the proper approvals," he said. "Plus, it's not like the place is fenced in or anything. It's only off limits because the military doesn't want anyone vandalizing all the old buildings."

Just then, a telephone company truck pulled up to the pumps. *Thank goodness*. I didn't need my dad wondering why we were suddenly so fascinated with a restricted Air Force base, especially if we *weren't* going there.

Dad told me to have fun, stay out of trouble, and be back before dark. That wouldn't be a problem. In the winter, "dark" would have meant half past four in the afternoon, but it was July and the sun didn't go down until after nine. So we had tons of time to get into – I mean, stay *out* of trouble.

Dad attended to his customer, and we left Sultana in the same direction the van had gone.

"We're making good time," I said, looking at my watch. "It only took us an hour and we're almost there." In Manitoba, the wind usually comes from the west, and this morning that made our lives easier by pushing us gently down Highway 45, toward Impact Lake.

Eric nodded and stopped pedaling. We had reached the highest point in the area and could now enjoy a long coast toward the east. You probably wouldn't even notice the decline in a car, but on a bike it was a relaxing roll for over a mile.

"Did you know that there *wasn't* a fence around the old base?" he asked.

"No. I always thought the place was like a jail, with a tall security fence and curly barbed wire up top. If I knew we could just walk in there, I would have checked it out a long time ago."

"I sure wish I had paid more attention to what that old guy said on our field trip."

"The one to the air museum?"

Eric nodded. "I bet that tour guide could have asked those divers some perfect questions – you know, to see what they really knew about planes."

"But like I said before, it might not even be planes they're after. It could be some other sunken object ... or ... or meteorites."

"Oh yeah," Eric beamed. "That's why it's called *Impact* Lake. Never mind a car tire exploding – can you imagine seeing that meteorite slam into the earth?"

I laughed. "I don't think I would want to be within a hundred miles of Impact Lake when that meteorite hit."

"Imagine how cool it would be to hold a chunk of rock that whizzed through the galaxy for billions of years," Eric said dreamily.

"Or one that came from some alien planet light years away."

"Yeah, it sure would be neat to find some meteorites," Eric said. "I wonder if they're worth any money. Maybe we could sell some of the ones we find."

"My dad told me a story once. He said that a guy was collecting rocks for a campfire pit, somewhere around here. And one of the rocks he picked up was unbelievably heavy for the size of the stone. So he took the rock to the museum in Winnipeg for testing and it turned out to be a meteorite."

"Sweet!" Eric said.

"And you know what else?"

"What?"

"He got fifty thousand dollars for that meteorite."

"Holy smokes! Fifty thousand!" Eric's bike wobbled dangerously, but he wrestled with the handlebars and steadied himself again. "We definitely have to look for some meteorites while we're there. And this time we're doing what we want with that money."

"You got that right!" I said.

The twenty-five thousand dollars we had received for creating our authentic-looking Egyptian tablet was divided equally into three and then promptly deposited into some sort of university education bank account. Sure, we each got one hundred dollars – *big whoop* – but the rest was immediately stashed away for when we graduated from high school. We had planned on buying important things right away – stuff like new bikes and metal detectors and computers – not stupid textbooks when we were old. *What a rip-off!*

We pedaled again for another few miles, until Eric stopped me. "There's their van," he announced, pointing to a speck in the distance.

Eric pulled off the asphalt and let his bike roll over to their empty trailer. I followed him to the grassy area where hunters, fishermen, and hikers parked their vehicles. The government didn't want anyone using the old approach road, so they prevented vehicle access by placing five giant boulders across the start of the trail to the lake. And as if that wasn't enough of a deterrent, a huge faded sign warned, ACCESS TO IMPACT LAKE BASE PROPERTY RESTRICTED TO AUTHORIZED PERSONNEL – DEPARTMENT OF NATIONAL DEFENCE.

I studied the sign with Eric. "But if there's no fence," I said, "how are people supposed to know where the base property begins – or ends?"

Eric scratched his head. "Yeah, no kidding. And why should that lady and those grouchy divers get to go there, but not anyone else. It's not fair."

I read the warning two more times. I felt as if it were daring us to go to the base. "On the other hand," I said, "if there isn't a fence, we'll have a solid excuse if we get caught hanging around the base."

"How's that?"

"Okay, check this out," I said. "So imagine we get caught. We say we were on our way to Elbow to go fishing, but when we got here – to this point on the highway – we decide to go fishing at Impact instead."

Eric nodded.

"Then, when we got to Impact Lake we became

disoriented and ended up at the base. If anyone catches us there, we say, 'Sorry, we're lost.'"

Eric's head bobbed up and down. "It's good that we have the fishing stuff too," he said. "Because it really looks like that's what we're doing."

"And remember, it's not illegal to fish in the lake, only to be on the base – at the west end of the lake." I pointed at all the tracks in the dirt from other hunters and fishermen. "And I bet we aren't the only ones who have checked out the base."

"We may as well take our bikes as far down the trail as we can," Eric said. He dug out a water bottle and took a few swallows.

I took off my backpack, pulled out one of my bottles, and had a drink too. "We should be there in half an hour or so."

Man, was that wishful thinking.

After more than seventy years of neglect, the road didn't feel much like a road anymore. I'm sure it used to be wide and solid, for all the heavy supply trucks that would have come from Winnipeg, but it was in terrible shape now. Huge poplar, spruce, and pine trees rose up all over the place, forcing us to ride super slow so we could weave around their thick trunks. On an all-terrain vehicle – an ATV – it would have been a hoot, but on bicycles it was a lot of work.

And after half a mile, things got worse.

"Where's the road?" Eric said, suddenly coming

to a stop.

I pulled up next to him. "Holy cow!" I said. "It's totally washed out." We were up on a rise and looking at a small creek forty feet below us. The road began again a hundred feet across the washout.

"But how can that be? There's only a trickle of water down there."

"Well, it didn't necessarily erode this week – or even this year. It might have washed away five or ten or fifteen years ago."

"Oh yeah, I keep forgetting this road hasn't been used by cars and trucks in decades."

"Should we go back?" I asked.

"Heck no," Eric shot back. "It's not a big deal. Those guys drove through here – the tracks are still fresh – and we can too." He pointed at the crisp dents left on either side of the creek by knobby tires.

We got off our bikes and pushed them down the zigzag path left by the ATVs. The quads had pounded a pretty good trail into the gully sides over the years and we probably could have ridden our bikes. But our backpacks limited our maneuverability and we didn't want to risk tumbling over. At the stream, I washed my face and then pushed my bike up the other side, to where the road resumed. We tried to pedal for another ten minutes – then gave up. The trail was so rough, it would be easier just to walk.

"This is pointless," Eric said, reading my mind. He got off his bike and pushed it into the forest.

"You got that right." We stashed our bikes carefully under the shrubs, so the divers – or anyone else, for that matter – wouldn't spot them. I marked the location next to the old roadbed with a rusty, punctured can that someone had used for target practice. I looked behind me at least ten times as we left the area, to make sure the bikes weren't visible from the trail, and to be certain I'd recognize the place on the way back. Satisfied that we could find our bikes again, we continued on *our* expedition to find the real purpose of the *diver's* expedition.

We walked in silence for another quarter mile, until we started seeing lots of rocks and boulders along the side of the trail. "Yes," Eric hissed with delight. "Meteorites!"

Eric and I began lifting and dropping rocks. We didn't have any proper testing equipment, so the best we could do was judge each rock by its weight in relation to the other rocks we picked up. In other words, we were looking for rocks that looked unusual and felt super-heavy – like the rock in Dad's story.

I was getting pretty hot, and after fifteen minutes of hoisting stones and dropping them, I stopped. Eric lasted a bit longer than I did, but he gave up eventually too. At least I thought he gave up. I saw him pick up a toaster-sized rock with both hands and throw it against a boulder – like he was mad.

"Whoa!" he screamed. "Cody! I think this might

25

be something."

I ambled over to him and looked at the dark gray rock sitting on the roadbed.

"Try and pick that one up," he ordered. "It weighs a ton. Seriously."

I tried to lift it with one hand but couldn't.

"I wanted to crack it open on that other rock," he said, panting. "But I couldn't even chip it. It *must* be from outer space."

I dug both hands under the chunk and picked it up. "Wow," I marveled, "it's at least three times heavier than all the other stones that are the same size."

"Told ya."

I turned over the piece and examined it some more. "But just because it's heavy doesn't mean it's from outer space. It could just be a chunk of steel – man-made steel." I hated to burst Eric's bubble, but the more I looked at the slab, the more it looked like metal.

"I sure hope it's a meteorite," Eric said. "I'll keep the first one I find and sell the others. We could buy some pretty cool stuff with fifty thousand dollars."

"It's way too heavy to pack around all day," I said. "Leave it here and we can pick it up on the way back."

Eric was worried the divers might find his prize, so he covered the rock with moss and marked the spot with some other stones.

Both of us were determined to get to the lake and find those divers, but we also didn't want to pass up the chance to grab a few valuable meteorites on the way. So we continued to scoop and examine rocks as we hiked down the trail.

After my thirtieth rock – *yup, I was counting them* – I said, "What's Rachel up to today?" Eric's sister had accompanied us on our zany holiday to Egypt and I had grown used to having her around.

"She's probably still mad at me," Eric said.

"Huh? Why would she be mad at you?"

"Because," he said slowly, "I told her that we *didn't* want her to come fishing with us today."

"WHAT?" I said, a lot louder than I'd meant to. I tried to control my voice. "Why would you tell her that?"

"I don't know. Anyway, it's more fun when it's just you and me – like in the old days."

I didn't say anything. I didn't have a sister, so I couldn't say what it was like having someone always wanting to do stuff with you – especially a girl. I just wish he hadn't said that *I* didn't want her along. It was bad enough that Eric didn't want her around for the day, but why'd he have to get me involved? *Jeez.*

Eric changed the subject. "Why would the Air Force build a training base way out here anyway? Impact Lake seems like a dumb spot."

"It's a dumb spot now," I said, "but it was a good spot in 1940."

"What difference does the year make?" Eric hopped over a fallen tree. The narrow quad trail

27

made by hunters and fishermen made a wide detour around the monstrous log. I suppose there were some advantages to being on foot.

I followed Eric over the tree. "Back then," I said, "the government planned on abandoning the old Trans-Canada Highway and building a new #1 highway, right through Sultana and all the way to Ontario. In fact, it would have been the only road linking Ontario and Manitoba. Anyway, they ended up scrapping the northern route – the one near here – and now the highway runs between West Hawk Lake and Falcon Lake."

"How do you know that? And what does that have to do with the Impact Lake base?"

"My dad has an old book on the history of the area. I read it while I was waiting for him to finish work – guess I was bored."

Eric shook his head. "I still don't get the connection between the base and the road." He stopped, picked up a rock, quickly assessed it for meteorite-ness, and tossed it aside.

"I'm getting to that," I said, picking up my own specimen and dropping it. "Impact Lake is smack in the middle of Canada. Apparently, the Air Force couldn't afford to operate two floatplane training schools in Canada. So they decided on locating *one* base strategically."

Eric took off a shoulder strap and twisted his backpack around so he could reach inside without taking the bag completely off. He groped in his pack and extracted two granola bars. "What's so strategic about this place?" Eric passed one bar to me and pointed down the road with the other one.

"Well," I said, removing the wrapper, "because Impact Lake was right in the middle of the country, they could quickly send trained pilots to the west or east coast – wherever they needed them. And with the main supply route *expected* to be only three miles from the base, I guess it made sense to them at that time."

Eric walked and chewed and seemed to consider my brief history lesson on the lake. "What about all those crazy rumors about ghosts and mad trappers and –" Eric broke off and stopped walking. "Hey! The quad tracks disappeared. It's like ... it's like they just vanished."

CHAPTER 2

I sidled up next to Eric, still munching on my snack. "Huh?"

"The trail from their ATVs – it's gone." Eric pointed at the old roadbed. We hadn't noticed it until now, but stretches of the access route made use of the natural granite bedrock that lay exposed along the way. We knew we were still on the road because all the big fissures and cracks were filled in with crushed rock. But the tracks we had been following were no longer visible.

I looked around and tried hard to listen for the sound of ATVs, but all I heard was the wind whistling up in the spruce trees. "Do you think they turned off this road and went down one of those hunting trails we passed?"

Eric turned and frowned at the stretch of road we had just covered. I knew him well and suspected he'd want to just keep moving forward.

"I don't feel like backtracking," he said. "We've got to be pretty close to the lake now."

"Yeah," I agreed, "that sure felt like three miles."

"And it doesn't matter if they did take a detour or some old service trail to get to the base. As long as we can find the base, we'll catch up to them."

"And maybe we'll even beat them there," I added. "That would be cool."

We continued south along the road, always scanning the ground for ATV tracks. We gave up on our quest for meteorites – for the time being, at least – and instead focused on finding the divers and the researcher. We saw lots of older tire treads heading into the woods, but not the crisp impressions left by their ATVs.

Where could they have gone?

Finally, we knew we were close. Not because we saw buildings or abandoned airplanes, but because of the sign. We both froze.

The giant metal warning was as big as any billboard and it repeated the threat we saw near the highway. Except this sign had a map in the middle and an extra line at the bottom that read, ACCESS TO IMPACT LAKE RESTRICTED TO EAST HALF – FAILURE TO COMPLY WILL RESULT IN ENFORCEMENT ACTION – DND.

"If we get caught out here," I said, "it's going to be hard to convince anyone we didn't see *that*."

Eric nodded. He reached way up and stuck his finger through one of the many bullet holes riddling the sign. "I guess no one likes to be told where they can't go."

"Especially hunters," I said.

"I wonder what 'enforcement action' means?"

"Whatever it is, it doesn't sound like fun. Maybe

we should just stick to the legal side." I pointed at the map of Impact Lake.

"We could," Eric said. "But it's a huge lake. We're not going to see a thing from the east shore. We might as well not even bother going then."

"I suppose if it's restricted to prevent vandalism – and we're *not* going to vandalize anything – we can't get into too much trouble. Plus, I really want to know what they're diving for."

"That makes sense to me," Eric said. "If they're going to pull a giant, billion-dollar meteorite from the lake, I want to be there."

We continued forward silently into the *RESTRICTED ZONE*. After a few more corners in the road, we began to see buildings. First a few garage-type sheds, then larger shops, and even a generator building with a corroded fuel tank next to it. Trails, walkways, and service roads fanned out all over the place.

Eric stopped at one of the major intersections. "Let's see where this path goes," he suggested, pointing down a road that looked like it hadn't been used since the 1940s.

Ten minutes later, Eric stopped suddenly. "Rats!"

I laughed when I saw what he was exclaiming about. We were staring at what was obviously the garbage dump for the base. Most of the area was overgrown with vegetation, but the rusted heaps of scrap metal, tires, glass, and tin cans still sat where they were dumped during the war.

I walked over to a mountain of glass the size of a car. "I guess they didn't have plastic back then." I picked up one of the bottles in the pile that wasn't smashed.

"Or recycling," Eric added. He poked through the hill with me for a minute. "We should come back here some time and go through this stuff. I bet a collector would pay good money for one of these pop bottles." Eric passed me a small bottle with a pebbled surface that looked pretty interesting.

"Yeah, this is neat," I said. "I've never seen anything like it." I placed the bottle at the base of a nearby tree so that we wouldn't have to look for it again if we returned.

We left the dump and began our hike back to the main intersection of roads and trails.

Something in the forest, off to the right, grabbed my attention. It was a bucket from an old bulldozer. I stopped and stared at the giant shovel in the distance. I think subconsciously my brain was trying to figure something out. But I couldn't be bothered waiting for my brain, so I walked over to the bucket and climbed in to study the scoop.

"I think I found your meteorite, Eric," I said, pointing at the front of the blade.

"What?" Eric had followed me and was now looking over the bulldozer bucket.

"It's just one of the teeth from this thing," I said.

Eric ran his fingers over the leading edge of the bucket. Most of the remaining teeth were severely dented and bashed up, but a few were totally missing. And those missing chunks were the same size as Eric's meteorite. He frowned. "I knew it was too good to be true."

We returned to the road and eventually arrived back at the crossroads.

"This time you pick a path," Eric said.

"Well," I said, indicating another road, "this one looks like the second most used trail. Let's try it."

We continued to scan for signs of the divers as we walked, but there was almost no point. Off-road vehicle tracks were everywhere. Some were older, some were newer – but they had overlapped and tangled together, and it was impossible to tell the direction anyone had traveled. It would be easier for us to find the lake first.

And we did.

We walked around a sharp corner on the road and suddenly there it was – the Impact Lake float-plane training base. And it was a lot bigger than I thought it would be.

"Excellent!" Eric whispered. We were both very nervous about getting caught so we decided to approach the center of the base quietly. We'd learned from our previous adventures that you never knew who might be watching.

We prowled around the smaller buildings,

heading for the water sparkling between the trees. Eric and I passed a long log structure and a bunch of other cabins – we decided to explore those next – and went straight to the docks. If divers really were going to haul a floatplane from the lake, we didn't want to miss it. And if they were lying to us and going to recover an enormous meteorite, a trunk full of cash, or some other treasure, we wanted to witness that too.

"This place is so cool," I said quietly. "The only thing missing is those old planes – and the people, I guess." We both crouched behind a service shed, scanning the waterfront area for the divers and the researcher, or any other sign of life.

"Yeah," Eric said, "I thought for sure all these buildings would be burned down, or collapsed, or ruined. But even the timbers on the dock look solid."

"I sure hope they turn this place into a Historic Site," I said. "Everyone should be able to come out here and look around."

"It would definitely be a destination for tourists to visit. *A real destination.*"

I nodded, knowing exactly what he meant. Sure, our tablet had stirred things up for a while, but people were already starting to forget about our hoax. The area needed a proper, permanent attraction. Then people would come all the time and on a regular basis. Plus, Impact Lake was only a fifteen minute car ride from Sultana, and Sultana was the only town for miles. So, if the floatplane training base were to become a Historic Site, it would definitely save Sultana ... for good.

I continued scanning the shoreline with the binoculars. "Where are they?" I passed the glasses to Eric for a look.

"If they aren't here," he said, "we might as well check out the pier." Eric left our hideout and boldly walked over to the dock.

I winced, wishing he'd be a bit more discreet. Just because the base was deserted didn't mean we should abandon all caution. Eric tested the heavily-treated planks by delicately stepping on the first few. When he realized they would hold his weight, he ran to the end of the fifty-foot pier.

I reluctantly followed Eric onto the dock. I stared down at the water, letting my eyes follow a thick post until it vanished eight feet below. The rumors were true. The lake was both deep and clear.

That was when I caught a movement out of the corner of my eye. I turned to the left, toward the long central building, but couldn't see anything there. I could have sworn I had seen something drift around the structure. I stared at the corner of the building without blinking until my eyes hurt. *Man, I'm jittery.*

Eric yanked me away from my thoughts. "Are you coming or what?" He waved me to the end of the dock and we both sat down between two steel tie-down rings that were bolted to the planks. They were probably used to secure the floatplanes.

Eric must have sensed I was anxious about getting busted. "Don't worry, Cody," he said, trying to assure me. "The place is abandoned and we're the only ones here. And if there is someone else here – other than the divers and the researcher, of course – they're in just as much trouble as us. Coming here was definitely worth the risk. The base is awesome. I wish we'd come before!"

I nodded enthusiastically, but I wasn't totally convinced. Someone – maybe the divers or the researcher – could be watching us right now. I pushed that frightening thought from my mind, shook off my backpack, and set it down next to me. Our feet dangled over the side, but they were still a foot above the lake. I wanted to feel how cold the water was, so I rolled onto my stomach. By leaning way over and stretching my arms, I managed to dip my hand into the water. "It's freezing!" I yanked my fingers from the icy lake.

Eric laughed and waited for me to sit up again. "You know," he said, "I think I'm getting hungry."

"You're always hungry. But eating something is a good idea." I pulled out a peanut butter sandwich, unwrapped it, and took a bite.

"What kind of sandwich is that?"

"Peanut butter." I knew *exactly* where this was headed.

"Is it good?" he asked.

37

"Very," I said.

"Uhhm ..."

"– Jeepers, Eric." I passed him the other half of my sandwich. "I told you to make a lunch – for the fishing trip."

Eric bit into the corner of the sandwich – my sandwich – and half of it disappeared in a second. After he finished swallowing, he said, "Thanks. You know how much I hate making sandwiches."

"Well, what did you pack to eat then?" I turned around and reexamined all the buildings along the lakefront, keeping an eye out for whatever I had seen earlier. *Nothing.*

Eric grinned. "Six granola bars and half a bag of cookies."

"Those cookies better be chocolate chip," I said, "and not those disgusting, dried-out oatmeal things."

Eric laughed. Together we ate his cookies – they were the tasty chocolate chip ones – and continued to scan the lake. Impact Lake was roughly two miles long and half a mile wide. The shoreline around the lake was made mostly of granite and other rock. It didn't look like it had any nice sand beaches like Lake Winnipeg did.

"I wonder where those three are?" Eric mumbled.

"Yeah, you would think the base here would be their starting point." I looked behind me at the twenty or more wartime buildings. *Just like a ghost town*, I thought. It was weird to be in a place that had so many buildings and residences, but no people anywhere. In the forest there were no people, but that was normal. Here, in the middle of what looked like a mini town, there wasn't a soul around. Only dozens of buildings staring at me with giant boarded-up windows that looked like eyes.

Eric yanked me from my daydream. "If that lady is researching this place," he said, "she should be here somewhere."

I pushed the spooky thoughts from my head and focused on our mission again. "And since the divers don't have a boat or a canoe, they must plan on diving from the shore."

"And I thought those floatplanes crashed at this end of the lake." Eric indicated the water around the pier with his bottle. "That is, if they're even looking for a floatplane."

"Yup, that's what I always thought too. The meteorite hit the earth somewhere out there." I pointed at the half of the lake closest to us. "The strike made a four-hundred-foot-deep dent in the ground. And that's where the planes are – at least that's what everyone always said."

"And that's why they never recovered the planes during the war," Eric added, confirming what I had heard too. "It was way too deep for divers back then."

"Hey!" I said. "I just thought of something else."

"What's that?"

"Well, if those guys *really* are going to recover a plane from the bottom of the lake, wouldn't they need a crane or a barge and a lot more people?"

Eric considered that for a minute and then nodded. "To get the plane right out of the water, they'd definitely need help. But to just find the plane and lift it – yeah, I think the two of them could do that. I saw a TV show where divers were raising cannons with air bags. They tied the bags on the cannons and then filled the bags with air from their tanks. The cannons floated to the surface like balloons."

"That sounds pretty cool." I glanced behind me again, this time at a giant hangar. Steel tracks led from the water to the shop that probably serviced the planes. "Those three should be here by now ..."

"What are you looking at?" Eric asked, squinting at me.

"I know this sounds stupid," I said, "but I think someone might be watching us."

Eric's eyes widened, but he kept his cool. He slowly turned back to face the lake. "Why do you think that?"

"Well," I said, staring out over the water again. "When I took off my pack and sat down here, I looked back and thought I saw someone duck behind the wall of one of the buildings. It's probably nothing, but I still have that feeling – the feeling we're being spied on."

"Could it be those divers?" Eric said excitedly.

"Or that researcher lady?"

"Maybe, but why would they sneak around? They're allowed to be here, remember. We're the ones who are breaking the law. Plus, those guys don't seem like they would sneak around. More likely, they'd tell us to scram – and they'd do that right to our faces."

"Maybe it's the ghost of one of those pilots, or the crazy trapper, or –"

"The ghost story is just a ghost story," I said. "It's schoolyard nonsense." Eric and I had heard variations of the pilot-ghost-tale for years. The rumor was that the pilots who drowned and died in their sunken planes continued to haunt Impact Lake and torment fishermen. Anyone who has ever hooked a big trout that got away has blamed ghosts for cutting the line. I sort of believe in spirits and stuff – just not in the Impact Lake ghosts, if you know what I mean. I found it hard to believe that just because someone drowned a place was haunted. If every lake where someone had a swimming accident became possessed with evil spirits, no one would ever go swimming or boating – including me.

"Okay, okay," Eric said, "but what about the mad trapper then? I'm sure he's real. People swear they've seen him."

"True," I admitted reluctantly. "It could be the trapper who's watching us. Or maybe, I'm just seeing things – imagining I saw something." I didn't really like the idea that an insane trapper was lurking around, and I think I preferred the notion that my mind was playing tricks on me.

But Eric wasn't quite done with his mad trapper theory. "Emma Betsill said she overheard two high school boys talking about him – about the trapper. They said they were hunting grouse on the east end of the lake when a hairy, seven-foot tall man came out of the forest and chased them away. His jacket was made of furs and leather, and he wore an old army helmet."

"Why would a trapper wear an old army helmet?" I said.

"Because he's crazy. Why else?" He turned his head quickly and searched the buildings along the edge of the lake. "I don't see anyone ..."

"We could split up and search the camp in opposite directions," I said. "You know, to try and catch the person, or to see if there even is a person."

"Are you kidding?" Eric said, standing up. "Don't you watch scary movies? As soon as *anyone* separates from the group in a horror movie, that person is toast – dead. Separating is the last thing we should do."

"Okay, okay," I said, getting up too. Now *he* was starting to freak *me* out. "We'll stick together."

The two of us couldn't just sit around all day waiting for the lady and the divers to show up. So we decided to explore some of the structures around the base, beginning with what we thought was the main training building. I slipped my pack on and followed Eric off the pier.

"I sure hope it's not locked," Eric said five minutes later. "It would be neat to look around in there."

We were now standing at the bottom of a wide set of steps that led up to a covered porch. I pointed at a white-washed boulder near the stairs. Peeling black letters still identified the building as the *MESS HALL*. We knew that was a military way of saying cafeteria. The porch ran along the entire length of the dining hall and provided a great view of the lake. I could easily imagine pilots and mechanics relaxing here after supper, telling stories and joking around, or just looking out over the beautiful lake.

I was as curious as Eric was to explore the old base, but I was also becoming nervous about getting caught. Or worse, getting caught on the base by someone *crazy*. I took a last anxious look around and then followed Eric up the wide, creaky steps.

The metal sign above the door was faded but we could still make it out: RCAF/BCATP IMPACT LAKE FLOATPLANE TRAINING STATION NO. 456.

"I wonder what BCATP stands for," Eric whispered, still studying the sign.

"We'll have to look that up on the Internet later." We knew a little bit about the Royal Canadian Air Force from a field trip to the *Manitoba Museum of Aviation*, but neither of us had heard of the BCATP before.

The windows were all sealed with planks of wood, but the door was uncovered – as if someone used it regularly. I fully expected the door to be locked but I elbowed Eric anyway, indicating he should check. He reached out, grabbed the old-fashioned brass doorknob, and gave it a twist.

It turned.

"I can't believe it!" Eric whispered, opening the door an inch. "It's not locked."

"Do you think *all* the buildings are unlocked – the barracks, the hangars, all of them?"

Eric shrugged and pushed the door open another three inches. He peeked inside.

"Let me see," I said, pulling him back.

Eric stepped aside and I stuck my head in the room. It was dark and I had to let my eyes adjust to the gloom. After a minute I still couldn't see anything, so I pushed the door open all the way. I now saw about ten feet of wood-plank flooring, but nothing else. It was simply too dark with all the windows boarded shut.

"We could sure use some flashlights," I whispered.

"Did you bring yours?" Eric asked.

"Why would I bring a flashlight to go fishing?"

Eric laughed. "Oh yeah, I forgot we weren't planning on coming here." He shuffled from foot to foot on the porch. "Should we go in anyway ... look around a bit?"

"What's the point?" I said, sneaking a peek behind me. *Gosh I was getting paranoid.* "We won't be able to see anything without lights. Well, except for that mousetrap." I pointed at the old-style, spring-loaded trap sitting on the floor against the wall.

Eric reached into the room and groped around on the wall for a light switch. His hand found something and I heard him flick it a few times. The power probably hadn't flowed through the wires for decades, but it was worth a try, I suppose. He shrugged and said, "Oh well, I guess we'll have to –"

SLAM!

Eric jerked his hand back. "Did you just hear something?" he whispered.

"Yeah," I said, swallowing hard. "It sounded like a door closing somewhere inside the building."

I quickly reached past Eric and pulled our door shut too, except I tried hard not to make any noise. We retreated down the stairs and ran north toward the nearest building. Both of us skidded around the corner and out of sight. When I caught my breath again, I stuck my head out and watched the mess hall. We were far enough away that we could see three sides of the building. That helped me relax a bit. I didn't want anyone leaving the mess hall and sneaking up on us without us seeing them first.

"Okay," Eric said, leaning against the wall and puffing. "Something weird is definitely going on around here."

"Yeah." I nodded. "Whoever's closing doors doesn't seem to want us snooping around."

Eric wiped his sweaty forehead with his wrist. "Maybe it was the ghost of –"

"– Enough about ghosts already," I said, searching among the buildings for any sign of movement. "A ghost didn't close that door. A ghost wasn't spying on us. And a ghost did *not* set that mousetrap."

"Huh?" Eric turned and looked at me. His face was still flushed with excitement. "What about the mousetrap?"

"There's no way that trap stayed set like that since 1940 – *without* catching a mouse. I think someone set it recently, and that must be who's watching us."

CHAPTER 3

"Whoa!" Eric said. He stared thoughtfully at the mess hall. "But maybe this place has a grounds-keeper, or security guard, or maintenance man?"

"That's possible," I said. "Although why wouldn't they just reveal themselves and come and talk to us – tell us to scram. We're the ones who aren't supposed to be here."

Eric peeked over my shoulder at the building we just ran away from. "And where are those stupid divers and that researcher? Could they have been shooed off by the same person who's slamming doors?"

"I don't think those divers were scared off – not that easily. And they wouldn't be interested in the buildings anyway, just the lake and ... Wait a minute! What if *they* are the ones who set the mousetraps?"

"You think?" Eric said, still studying the mess hall.

"Well sure. Those three had lots of time to zip around the base and set traps."

"But why? What would they want with a bunch of dead mice?"

I shrugged. "Maybe they're poachers. Maybe they found a special buyer – some crazy rich dude – who wants his socks made from mouse fur. Who knows?"

"Let's wait here for a while and see if anyone leaves the mess hall," Eric suggested.

I agreed that was a good idea and together we kept an eye on three of the five entrances to the central building.

After twenty minutes of silence, Eric said, "Do you suppose it's possible that the wind closed the door? Maybe no one was in there with us."

"It did look like a pretty drafty place, didn't it? Maybe when we opened the outside door, we created a breeze that closed an inside door."

Now we both felt a bit silly for being so jumpy. But we still watched the mess hall carefully for another five minutes.

"Let's go," Eric finally said. "I think we're just getting spooked, that's all."

We decided to begin hiking back to the old road, and to stop and check out the buildings on the way.

The first structure was either a laundry or shower house – it was hard to say which. The building was the size of a two-car garage and it had the same corrugated metal roof as all the others. The doors were missing and many of the windows were smashed, so we could easily see what was inside. Only there wasn't much to see inside. There were lots of water pipes and floor drains, but everything was so mangled, it was hard to imagine what anything was used for.

"Check it out," I said, pointing behind a stack of

pipes. "Another mousetrap."

"And there's another one." Eric pointed to the opposite wall. "Both are still set – ready to go."

We left the shower-house, or whatever it was, and walked farther away from the mess hall. The more distance we put between *that* building and us, the more comfortable we felt. I was almost certain the wind had knocked a door shut, but if I was wrong … I shuddered nervously at the thought.

Eric picked up his pace, guiding us toward the road that led to the base. And that was when we discovered the last building. We'd almost missed it entirely, but Eric noticed the structure when he left the gravel path we were on to stop for a pee break. The shed was hidden deep in the forest, on the fringe of the base.

"I wonder why that building's so far from all the other ones," Eric said.

We moved through the pine trees toward the shop – or whatever it was. When we got close enough to see the whole building, I realized it was an exact copy of the hangar down by the pier. It even had the massive sliding doors that made up the entire west side. But it didn't make much sense that the floatplanes would be serviced this far from the water, especially since they already had a hangar right next to the lake.

"Crazy place to store a floatplane," Eric said, reading my mind.

"Maybe it was for a top-secret experimental plane." I pointed at the sign over the door. "Look."

Eric read the warning out loud. *"Building strictly off-limits to unauthorized personnel.* Even if it was for a test plane, why wouldn't they keep it by the other hangar?"

"My dad always says that the military does pretty illogical stuff. I suppose this might be an example of that – if it really was for a plane, I mean."

"Only one way to find out," Eric said, boldly stomping off to try the door on the side of the hangar.

I glanced behind me to make sure we weren't being tailed and then I followed Eric. Beyond the airplane hangar I saw a low depression that must have been used as a stone quarry for getting rocks for the base. The hole was the size of a football field and it looked like there was no end to the rocks they could have mined.

Eric paused when he got to the door and waited for me to catch up. The door didn't have a knob so we knew it wouldn't be locked. "You know what would be awesome?" Eric said.

"Yeah. If there was a floatplane inside."

"Exactly. Imagine if there was a plane inside this hangar that the Air Force forgot about when they closed the base. And imagine if we were the ones to discover it? Those grumpy divers could dive their faces off looking for a sunken airplane and we'd be famous for discovering one right here – without even getting wet. We'd probably get a huge reward and –"

"Why don't we just see what's inside first," I suggested. "*Before* we get too excited."

Eric pulled on the heavy steel door and went in. "Darn!"

I grinned, guessing that meant there was no plane. "Too bad," I said.

Instead of a plane, there was just some kind of big machine. I walked past Eric, deeper into the building. The hangar was well lit because the top half of the giant sliding doors were made of glass, allowing in plenty of daylight.

Eric had followed me to the center of the room and we both stood staring at the odd-looking device. "What is that thing?" he wondered out loud.

"And why is it inside a hangar meant for airplanes?" I asked. The contraption was the size of a small car and it was made entirely of metal. A greasy-looking drum as big as a dishwasher gave the impression that the device might be some kind of printing press. But that didn't make sense either. A trough above the greasy wheel must have passed something over the roller.

Eric kicked a metal barrel marked BEEF TALLOW – whatever that was. "Could it be for crushing rocks?" Eric said. "To make gravel, maybe?"

Finely crushed gravel littered the concrete floor, so his guess seemed reasonable. "Could be," I said. "But I think I saw the rock crusher outside, near the edge of the quarry. I don't see anything on this machine for smashing rocks. It wouldn't make sense for them to bring stones inside here, just to smash them."

"I got it!" Eric cried. "It must be for finding meteorites. They took the rocks that they were going to use for the road, or walkways, or whatever, and hauled them in here to filter out the valuable meteorites."

I shrugged, not sure what to think. People had known, for a hundred years at least, that Impact Lake was partially formed by a meteorite crater. So I suppose it was possible that the Air Force wanted to find pieces of the original meteorite too. Space fragments were worth a lot of money now, and maybe they were worth a lot of money during the war.

"But why would they crush the rocks first?" I said. "Meteorites are more valuable if they're bigger. The rocks left on that conveyor are small. Who would want a bunch of baby meteorite fragments?"

This time Eric shrugged.

I followed him around the machine, wondering what its purpose was back in the 1940s. We spotted three more mousetraps set up along the outside walls.

A bunch of loose papers were on the floor and I picked one up. It was yellow, brittle, and about half the size of a regular sheet. A line at the top explained that it was FORM 2b: REQUEST FOR IMMEDIATE SUPPLIES and it was dated 10 June 1941. The letters were all a bit crooked like they were typed on one of those ancient typewriters that pressed the individual letters through an ink ribbon.

"Whatcha got there?" Eric leaned over my shoulder and studied the request. "Hmm ... Looks like Red Stevenson ordered the wrong stuff, huh?"

"I guess." The paper said that Red Stevenson wanted to buy three drums of aviation grease. At least that's what the requisition asked for. But the "aviation grease" was crossed out with typed Xs and replaced with "beef tallow." I didn't know much about either item, but I did think it was odd that someone confused grease for a floatplane with beef tallow. The request was signed C. POCHINKO, HQ, WINNIPEG. I put the document on the floor again.

Eric went over to a chest-high work table that had its own south-facing window. He ran his hand over a black piece of leather that was stretched across the work surface. The leather was now cracked and dusty, but the area under the window seemed to play an important role in whatever went on in the hangar. I was staring at the ugly, un-military-looking flower pattern on the tattered curtains when Eric interrupted my thoughts.

"Why would a shop like this be off limits to people working on the base," Eric mumbled, "when none of the other buildings were?"

"Yeah," I agreed, "it's pretty weird, all right. Unless whatever they were doing here was a huge secret – one we don't understand ... yet."

Eric nodded. "Such a huge hangar ..." he pointed at the machine in the middle of the floor, "for this funny-looking thing."

"Maybe they were experimenting with food." I copied Eric's habit of always kicking stuff and booted a ridiculously big cooking pot. It looked as if it could make chicken noodle soup for everyone in Sultana.

"No kidding." Eric hoofed the vessel as well. "You'd think these pots would be in the mess hall kitchen."

I glanced at my wristwatch. "I think we better get going. It'll take us three or four hours to get back to Sultana."

Eric nodded. "We can always come back and –"

SLAM! This time, the door to the hangar closed with a bang.

I spun around, but saw no one.

Eric looked at me wide-eyed and I knew he was thinking what I was thinking. *There's no way a breeze closed that big steel door!*

"Quick!" I said, pointing to a second door on the opposite wall. "Let's get out of here."

I ran to the door and sprinted outside. Our feet pounded across the quarry as we ran for cover behind the rusty rock crusher. We slid behind the mechanical hulk and tried to catch our breath.

"That door weighed a ton!" Eric said. "I had to use both hands to pull it open. The wind couldn't have done that."

"And there is no wind there – by the door," I said. "That corner is totally sheltered by the forest."

We peeked around the rock crusher and stared at the hangar.

"What's that?" Eric said.

My eyes focused on the spot where Eric was pointing. "What? What is it?" I didn't see anything.

"Near those oil drums," Eric said urgently. "A shadow ... something big ..."

"I see it!" I couldn't tell what it was, but I definitely saw it too. Old oil drums lay on their sides, piled up in the shape of giant pyramids. Between these metal pyramids stood a dark shadow.

"It looks like ..." Eric swallowed, "like someone's hiding there, or waiting."

"It's moving!" I whispered. The blurry form began to shrink as whoever it was headed off to the south – into the forest.

"This place is really giving me the heebie-jeebies now," Eric said. He shuddered and tried to rub the goose bumps off his arms. "It's no wonder the base got such a whacky reputation over the years."

Eric and I decided to continue our escape north and head back to the main road. Although we would have loved to find the lady and the divers and spy on them, we had no desire to run into anyone. And that included grouchy military police, mad trappers, creepy divers, mouse-poaching researchers, and malicious ghosts.

We left the quarry and hiked a wide arc around the hangar and the oil drums. After spending half an hour wandering the narrow forest trails, we finally found the abandoned access route for the base, and followed it north. Our bikes were where we'd left them – thank goodness. For a moment there, I had worried they would be gone. We took a short break at the washout and then pedaled the rest of the way to Highway 45. We were both stunned to see the van and the trailer still parked in the clearing next to the start of the old roadbed.

"This is all getting pretty weird," Eric said, staring at the empty trailer.

"Yeah." I nodded. "I actually thought they packed up and left." Just when I thought we might only be imagining things, everything became more mysterious. If the van and trailer had been gone, that would have explained why we didn't see the three strangers anywhere at the lake or the base.

Eric and I pedaled hard into the west wind, and by the time we crossed the bridge into Sultana, we were exhausted. The whole way back I had been going over the peculiar events of the day, and the more I thought about Impact Lake, the more confused I became. What were those divers really after? If they were after a sunken plane – like they claimed to be – why weren't they at the lake? And where was the researcher who was supposed to be researching the base? Who was spying on us, and why were they trying to scare us away? Why was someone poaching mice?

I enjoyed a good puzzle, but I was worried this might not be a puzzle I could solve. I'd seen how awesome the old base was and I wanted everyone to be able to visit the site. But I also really wanted Eric's mom to keep her job at the restaurant. I wanted the Impact Lake base to permanently do what our fake tablet only did temporarily. And I didn't want anything to mess that up.

"You wanna come in for a bit, or what?" Eric asked. He stopped his bike at the end of his driveway.

"Yeah, I want to ask Rachel something." I leaned my bike against the house and Eric dropped his on the lawn.

"What?" Eric said. "You think she can help us?"

"Maybe ... I'm not sure."

We didn't even need to go inside the house to find Rachel. When we got to the back door, we noticed her sitting at the picnic table in the backyard painting a picture. Her tubes of oils and brushes were spread out all over the table. She was working on an outdoor scene with trees, a river, teepees, and –

"Hey!" I said. "I recognize that. It's the Cree camp from old Sultana."

She smiled at me but deliberately ignored her brother.

She didn't seem to be mad at me, so I continued talking. "That looks really good, Rachel. There's the tree where we hid the walkie-talkie, there's the tent we stayed in, and that must be us."

Eric leaned over the table and studied the artwork. "Where am I? I don't see anyone that looks like me."

"You're picking berries," Rachel said.

"Where?" Eric scanned the painting again, looking for a berry picker.

"You're over here," she pointed to a spot on the picnic table that was off the canvas.

Eric laughed loudly. "Good one, Rachel. Next time you should find a bigger canvas. You're missing the most important person." Rachel scowled at him.

"Looks like you're almost done," I said, trying to ease the tension.

"Yeah," she said. "I had lots of time to paint because *no one* –" this time she glared at both of us – "wants to do anything with me."

I quickly tried to change the subject. "Hey, I got an e-mail from Anna this morning."

"Oh yeah?" Rachel's face brightened up a bit. "What did she say?"

I'd already told Eric about the e-mail I'd received from Anna when I saw him this morning. He hadn't seemed too interested at the time – I think he was still half asleep – but I knew Rachel would be.

"There's not that much to tell," I began. "Her message basically said that her dad and her uncle Rudi were working out the details for another project – an archaeological project, I guess. And they asked the three of us to join them."

"Wow!" Rachel said. "Did the letter say where they're going?"

I shrugged. "She didn't say where or when."

"I wouldn't get too excited," Eric said to his sister. "A dig could take months to organize."

"That's fine with me," Rachel said. "I'll gladly wait months – or even years – for the chance to go on a real archaeological dig." The idea of another trip seemed to melt away any remaining frostiness Rachel may have felt.

"Uhmm," I began, deciding to ask her the question I really had on my mind. "Do you remember in May when we went on that field trip to the air museum with the class?"

"Yeah, what about it?"

"I saw you take a bunch of pamphlets from the display when we first walked in the place. Do you still have them?"

"You took pamphlets from the museum?" Eric asked.

Rachel rolled her eyes. "That's what pamphlets are for – for visitors to take."

"I know *that*," Eric said, sitting down across from

her. "I just didn't think people actually took any."

"Well, I did," she said. "I thought it was an interesting place and I was glad Mrs. Leavesley took us there."

"Anyway," I interrupted. "Do you still have them – the brochures?"

"No," Rachel said, cleaning one of her brushes in a glass of dirty water.

"Oh." I found it hard to hide my disappointment. "That's too bad."

"But I read them all." Rachel smiled at me and wiped a smear of gray paint from her cheek. "What do you want to know?"

I sat down next to Eric. "First of all, do you know what the letters B-C-A-T-P mean?"

Rachel repeated the letters to herself quietly, and then said, "Yeah. That's *The Plan*."

"Huh?" Eric said.

"What's 'The Plan?'" I asked.

"The British Commonwealth Air Training Plan – the BCATP. During World War II everyone just called it 'The Plan.' It was a big deal in Canada."

"And you remember that from this piece of paper?" Eric asked.

"No," Rachel shook her head. "I remember *that* from when the tour guide, Mr. Davis, told us about it."

Eric took one of the paint brushes and pretended to paint his fingernails. "How come I don't remember that?"

"Because you guys were too busy running around looking at the planes. You never stayed close enough to Mr. Davis to hear all his terrific stories about the museum."

Eric snorted.

"What did he say about 'The Plan'? What was it all about –?"

Eric cut me off. "But please keep it short, Rachel."

Rachel ignored Eric. "During WWII," she began, "the skies over England were pretty cluttered with airplanes shooting each other and bombing stuff. In fact, Mr. Davis said it became so dangerous the Air Force decided to stop training pilots in England and decided instead to train all the new pilots in Canada."

"Why Canada?" I asked.

"We have lots of space and good flying weather. And in Canada there were no aerial dogfights – no shootouts with other planes – so it was safer."

"And Impact Lake was a training school, right?" Eric said.

"Yeah. One of about seventy in Canada." Rachel dried her brushes with a paper towel and placed them in a box.

"Whoa!" I said. "There were that many?"

"That's what Mr. Davis said. They had schools for pilots, schools for navigators, schools for observers, schools for bombers, and even schools for radio operators. There were lots of different training schools, each specializing in something."

"And the Impact Lake School specialized in training pilots to land and take off on floats," Eric said.

"Yup." Rachel nodded. "They would have learned how to fly a regular plane in Brandon, or Dauphin, or at some other base, but if they were going to fly floatplanes, they learned that at Impact Lake."

"Hmm." Eric looked at me thoughtfully. "I wonder how many floatplanes those new pilots crashed into the lake?"

"The *Sharks*?" Rachel said. "None."

"What sharks?" Eric asked. "There are sharks in Impact Lake?"

Rachel shook her head. "Are you guys kidding me?" She sounded frustrated. "Didn't you learn *anything* at the museum?"

Eric didn't seem fazed by his sister's sarcasm, but I was feeling pretty sheepish. The museum was a cool place and the class field trip had been a ton of fun. But Eric and I immediately slipped away from the cluster of classmates around the tour guide and headed off on our own to explore the planes. It sounded like we missed a lot of good information – information that could have helped us.

I stared down at Rachel's painting and kept my mouth shut.

After a minute of silence, Rachel explained. "The RCAF – that's the Royal Canadian Air Force – ordered twenty-three *Blackburn Sharks*. That's the name of the floatplane – a *Shark*. Anyway, seven planes were sent to Impact Lake as trainers, eight went to a base in British Columbia, and eight went to a base somewhere on the east coast. After the war all the *Sharks* were accounted for. In fact, *none* of the floatplanes saw any action during the war."

"But what about those floatplanes – those *Sharks* – that sank in the lake?" Eric asked.

"That's what I'm trying to tell you," Rachel said. "None of them crashed at Impact Lake – or anywhere, for that matter."

CHAPTER 4

"How do you know that?" Eric challenged.

Rachel sighed. "*Because* Mrs. Leavesley asked Mr. Davis the very same question. She asked if the rumors were true that there are planes at the bottom of Impact Lake. And Mr. Davis said the RCAF accounted for *all* their floatplanes after the base closed."

Eric and I stared at each other. I'm sure we were thinking the same thing. *What the heck were those divers up to?*

"What's with the goofy looks?" Rachel said, studying us.

I opened my mouth to fill her in, but Eric cut me off. "Nothing. We're just curious."

Rachel folded her arms across her chest. "Yeah, sure. You expect me to believe that you guys suddenly developed a keen interest in the history of World War II training bases."

"Yup," said Eric.

"Let's just tell her already," I said. We both knew we needed Rachel's help, but I think Eric liked to tease his sister and make her crazy with curiosity.

Eric handed Rachel the paint brush he'd been playing with. "What's the point?"

"She might be able to help us figure out what's

going on there," I said.

Rachel looked up at me. "'What's going on there?'"

"Exactly," I said.

"No." Rachel shook her head. "I mean, *what's* going on *where*? What are you talking about?"

"Oh. Eric and I went to Impact Lake today to follow a researcher and some suspicious scuba divers –"

"Why were they *suspicious*?" Rachel asked.

"Because they told us," Eric said, "that they were going to Impact Lake to dive for a type of plane that didn't even exist during WWII and –"

"But there are no sunken planes at Impact Lake," Rachel interrupted. "I just told you –"

"We didn't know *that* then." This time Eric cut in. "We thought there were planes in the lake. Anyway, we suspected they might be up to something, we just didn't know what. So we followed them – or tried to, at least."

Rachel frowned at a fly that decided to land on her painting and got stuck. "I wonder what they're doing there." She pulled the insect off carefully and released it.

"That's what we want to figure out," I said. We told Rachel about our day at Impact Lake – beginning with the conversation at the gas station with the strangers and ending with our suspicions about being watched.

Rachel sat across from me, thinking quietly. After

a minute she said, "Could that person – the person who you think was spying on you – have been one of the divers?"

"Sure," I said. "It's possible, but ..."

"But they're kind of nasty," Eric added. "If they didn't want us at the base, they would have walked up to us and told us to beat it."

"Yeah." I nodded. "They didn't seem very ... what-d'ya-call-it ... *subtle*?"

"And you never saw them anywhere at the base?" Rachel asked.

"Nope," Eric answered.

"And the researcher?" Rachel said. "You never saw her either?"

"Nope." That was Eric again.

"You think she's together with the divers – on the same team?" Rachel asked.

"I don't think so," I said. "My dad asked her that and she said she wasn't."

"She seems a lot less sneaky too," Eric said.

"Hmm." Rachel pondered the mystery we'd spent the day pondering. "Maybe the mad trapper was watching you guys."

Eric and I shrugged.

"I think that *we*," Rachel paused to make sure Eric and I understood "we" meant all of us this time, "should *all* go back to Impact Lake and find those three strangers. And when we find them, we should spy on *them* and find out what they're up to."

"But aren't you worried about running into whoever was spying on us?" Eric asked.

"No," Rachel said, "not really."

"Really?" I asked, surprised at her bravado.

Rachel looked at me and shook her head. "Well, no. I would be way more nervous about going back if someone had actually walked up to you and Eric and threatened to throw you in jail ... or ... or shoot you for trespassing."

"I never thought of it that way," I said.

Eric grinned at his sister, signaling he was okay with her hanging out with us again. "You might be a girl," he said, "but sometimes I like the way your brain works."

Rachel smiled at us. Coming from Eric, that was a huge compliment.

I didn't want to make a big deal out of it, but I was happy Rachel would be joining us. I felt like our team was together again, ready to solve another mystery – just like back in Egypt –

"– Well, Cody?" Rachel asked, pulling me back from my daydream.

"Huh?" I said.

She shook her head and sighed. "Boys really do have short attention spans. I *said* we should go to your house to do some more research on the base. It's too late to go back to the base today, so we might as well see if we can find clues about what those divers are up to."

By the time we got to my house it was after seven. I'd missed supper by an hour, but that was okay with me. Not only because the kitchen smelled like Mom's tomato and rice casserole – *yuck!* – but because I wasn't hungry anyway. I think I was too excited about the three of us tackling the mystery of Impact Lake.

Dad had left a sticky note on the fridge saying he and mom were having coffee over at Mr. and Mrs. Klock's house. Bonus, I thought. We would have the computer to ourselves.

Eric read the message over my shoulder, said "Excellent," and opened the fridge. If Mom and Dad were home he would never be so bold, but since they weren't, he felt he could do whatever he wanted. He grabbed the last can of root beer and carried it over to the computer. After a few swallows he let out a thunderous burp.

"Could you be any ruder?" Rachel asked, pulling up a chair.

Eric laughed. "If you want to hang out with us, sis, you need to accept us the way we are." He tried to force another burp, but it sounded more like a hiccup.

As soon as the Internet search engine appeared on the screen, I typed Impact Lake Floatplane Training Base.

Most of the time when we researched stuff, the first results that came up were the best. I clicked the top link, and connected with a page called BCATP SCHOOLS OF WWII. I prowled through the different indexes until I found a list of all the training bases in Canada. I spotted the Impact Lake base link and clicked on it.

"Perfect," Eric said.

We were all staring at a photo of the Impact Lake camp – complete with floatplanes, pilots, and mechanics. The picture was black and white, and obviously taken during the 1940s. Superimposed over the image were the words RCAF/BCATP IMPACT LAKE FLOATPLANE TRAINING STATION NO. 451.

"So that's what it looked like way back then," Rachel said. She sounded impressed.

"And that's pretty much the way it looks today," Eric said. "Except now it's overgrown with weeds and shrubs and trees, and there are no planes or people, of course."

Rachel shook her head. "It's so unfair that people aren't allowed to go there for a picnic – or just to walk around. It looks like such a neat place."

"That might change," Eric said.

"Why's that?" she asked.

"Cody's dad said that the lady we told you about was checking out the place – to make it a Historic Site."

"Sort of an open-air museum," I added. "Like Mit Rahina, in Egypt."

"Really?" Rachel said. "That would be terrific for

Sultana – for the whole area."

I left the photo up on the screen for a while. "Too bad it's all in black and white," I said after a few minutes. "It would be interesting to see the color of those planes." In the picture, four gray-looking float-planes were tied snug against the pier – the same pier Eric and I had sat on earlier today. I suppose the other three *Sharks* were flying around the lake or being serviced in the hangar.

"They're yellow," Rachel said.

"How do you know that?" I asked.

"Because they're *all* yellow."

"And *how* do you know that?" Eric said.

"Mr. Davis said that all the training aircraft in Canada were painted the same color – yellow. So these four would have been yellow too." Rachel looked back and forth between Eric and me. "Don't tell me you guys didn't notice all the bright yellow planes at the museum?"

"I thought the museum just liked yellow," Eric said. "I didn't know it was a rule or anything."

We looked at a few more pictures of the base from various angles, and then at some more photographs of the Blackburn Shark. It was an extremely cool looking biplane, with a lower wing running under the belly – just above the floats – and an upper wing propped up over the two-person covered cockpit.

Eric admired the image, but then shook his head. "And you're sure none of these crashed in the lake?" I

think he really wanted there to be one in the water –
so that we could find it.

"Yes," Rachel said. "They were all present and
accounted for after the war."

Under the pictures, near the bottom of the page,
we found a short summary of the history of the base.

----

*Although controversial from the beginning, Training
Station No. 451 was completed by the spring of 1940.
At the time, Impact Lake was harshly criticized by many
senior Air Force personnel as being an unfavorable
location. Despite this, the commissioned Base Commander,
Major Reginald Whiting, refused to consider alternate
sites. He stubbornly insisted Impact Lake was the best
place in Canada for a floatplane school and said he would
not operate one anywhere else.*

*In its three year operation, Training Station No. 451
graduated more than three hundred BCATP floatplane
pilots. But even with this impressive record, Impact Lake
could not escape accusations of questionable labor
management and cost overruns. Rumors of unusual base
activities and conspiracies continued until long after the
base closed.*

Rachel finished reading first. She leaned back in
the chair and folded her arms. "Hmm. Impact Lake
sounds like it was always an odd place."

"Yeah," I mumbled. "But to be honest, I didn't
really understand most of that."

"There are way too many big 'C' words," Eric complained. "'Controversial,' 'commissioned,' 'conspiracy' – how is any of that helpful?"

Rachel tapped on the second word. "'Controversial' means ... not everyone was happy with the base. 'Conspiracy' means something sneaky was going on. And 'commissioned' ... well, I don't know what that means."

"Look it up, Cody," Eric said, giving me an unnecessary poke in the ribs.

The online dictionary had five definitions for the word, but we were only interested in the military meaning. I studied the explanation and then waited for Rachel's interpretation.

"It sounds like a commission is something the army – or in our case, the Air Force – gives to someone to make an officer out of a regular person," she said.

I nodded. That was sort of what I gathered too.

Eric frowned. "You mean the Air Force can just take anyone and make them a captain or a major?"

"Well, not just *anyone*," I said. Eric had obviously skipped a few sentences. "It says that you have to have a university degree or some other skill the military needs."

"So this Major Whiting guy," Eric said, "wasn't in the Air Force all his life. He had some other job *before* the war started – *before* he started the floatplane base at Impact Lake."

"I guess so," I said.

"It sounds like it," Rachel added.

I closed the dictionary and returned to the photos of the old base. When I found the picture I was looking for, I expanded it so that it filled the whole screen. It was a group shot of at least fifty men. Judging by the camera angle, and the lake in the background, the photographer must have been up on the roof of the mess hall when he snapped it.

"I wonder if that's the major," Eric said, tapping a face in the back row. His finger left a condensation mark from his drink and I had to wipe it away to see the man.

"Probably," I said. The guy Eric had pointed to was wearing the most impressive uniform and he looked like he commanded respect. His weathered face had lots of wrinkles and I wondered briefly if his *normal* job involved doing stuff outside.

"These must have been the pilots," Rachel said, pointing at twenty young men who were grinning widely. If Eric and I got to fly those *Sharks* around, you better believe we'd be laughing too!

"And these were probably the mechanics who worked on the planes," Eric said, indicating the guys in coveralls who were sitting on chairs in the front row.

"Look!" I said. "They even had a base mascot." A boy roughly our age had a firm grip on some sort of terrier wearing a pilot's cap. The dog didn't look happy and I'm sure he shook off the cap the second the picture was taken.

Eric read the caption beneath the photograph out loud. *"Officers, pilots, and support personnel of the 4-5-1. Andalusian camp dog, Mickey, seen in foreground. 16 September 1940."*

"Too bad they don't identify all the men," Rachel said. "It would be fun to know their names."

"It would be even more fun," Eric said, "to go back to Impact Lake and find out what those divers are looking for."

"So let's go first thing tomorrow," Rachel said.

"Yeah," I said, shutting down the computer. "And the earlier we leave Sultana, the better."

Rachel gave Eric a good stare. "Did you hear that?" she asked.

Eric looked offended. "Hey, I was ready at nine this morning. Right, Cody?"

I laughed. "Yes, but we agreed to leave at eight."

"Don't worry, Cody," she said, "I'll make sure we're both here at seven-thirty sharp."

"Perfect," I said, and then wondered how *I* was going to get up that early.

We briefly discussed what kind of equipment and food we needed to take along. Eric was especially concerned about the quality and quantity of snacks we'd be taking. He felt that because we were leaving earlier, we'd need a lot more grub. Anyway, by nine o'clock we had everything figured out and I walked my friends to the door.

I watched them pedal down the street and began to fret about tomorrow's expedition. And I had that same feeling in my chest – as if an elephant was sitting on it – that I had in Egypt when we found out Eric would have to go through the pillars alone. But I also felt an urgent need to go back to Impact Lake and figure out what was going on at the base.

CHAPTER 5

The stuff I dreamt of that night made no sense at all. Visions of sunken treasure, mysterious spaceships, mousetraps, meteorites, and crashed airplanes all floated through my head. It was like watching bits and pieces of really bad movies. I suspected my brain was trying to sort through the mysteries of Impact Lake, but that didn't help me sleep any better.

My alarm clock went off at seven, saving me from a weird nightmare about a shaggy trapper chasing me while I pedaled like mad on my bike. I blinked a few times, turned off the alarm, and let my head flop back onto the pillow. A minute later my back-up clock began chirping. You see, I was so worried about sleeping in – and, yes, being one-upped by Eric – I'd set two alarms. *That was pretty darn smart of me*, I thought.

"– Hey, sleepy," a voice cut in, "I thought you and your friends were going fishing again this morning."

I opened an eye and glanced at my watch. Holy smokes – it was 7:15! I had fallen asleep again.

"Yikes!" I said, jumping out of bed and stumbling past my mom.

Mom shook her head and stepped out of the way. I gave my teeth a quick brush, splashed water on my face, and put on a clean T-shirt. In the kitchen – between mouthfuls of cereal – I explained to my mom that the three of us were going to Impact Lake today. "To the east end – the legal half," I said, letting her know we wouldn't be doing anything criminal.

Mom told me to have fun and to make sure I put lots of sunscreen on. She was never worried that I'd fall off my bike, or get West Nile Virus from a mosquito, or be eaten by a wolf, or drown in the river. But she always acted like I'd break out in skin cancer *instantly* if I stayed in the sun for more than five minutes without a thick layer of SPF 30. Once I agreed to thoroughly grease myself down, Mom said goodbye and took off for her job at the campground office. My dad had already left for work at the service station.

I had finished cramming my backpack with food by the time Rachel and Eric arrived. They were pedaling up the driveway, and I was tucking a flashlight in a side pocket, when I happened to glance out the kitchen window. True to Rachel's word, it was exactly half past seven. Eric looked like he had just woken up, but his sister looked alert. Her hair was neatly pulled back and restrained with a bright yellow elastic thing. And unlike her twin, she looked happy and excited.

I went outside and said, "Hi."

"Good morning," said Rachel.

Eric looked around, bewildered. "Gosh, it's

early," he said. "The grass is still wet with dew."

"Just ignore him, Cody," Rachel said. "He only got out of bed ten minutes ago."

"Really?" I swung my pack over a shoulder.

"Yeah, and I didn't even have breakfast yet," Eric whined. "Come to think of it, I didn't even pee yet."

Rachel scrunched her face in disgust. "Gross!"

"Well, at least you had time to get dressed," I said.

Rachel shook her head. "He slept in his clothes last night – to save time. Can you believe it?"

Eric laughed and walked over to the outside water faucet. "And by doing *that*," he said, "I was able to sleep an extra five minutes. In fact, grownups could save a lot of time in the morning if they wore their clothes to bed – *instead* of pajamas. I call that 'innovative thinking.'" Eric washed his face, rinsed his mouth, and turned off the tap again.

"And *I* call that being unbelievably lazy," Rachel countered.

We climbed on our bikes and headed east down the highway. It was too early for the wind to help push us along, but at least it wasn't hot out yet. And with zero traffic on the road it was a pleasant ride. Rachel and I pedaled side by side while Eric stayed behind us. He told us he could save energy if we broke wind and let him ride in our slipstream.

I told Rachel what to expect on the long ride to the base. Instead of being discouraged by my description of the beat-up road, she actually seemed excited.

"I can't wait to see that washout," she said. "It sounds impressive."

After about a mile, I turned around to see how Eric was doing. I nearly fell off my bike laughing. He had his backpack swung around so that it was against his stomach. The top flap was open and a cereal box was sticking out of the top. He had one hand on the handlebar, and with the other he was shoving fistfuls of Cheerios into his mouth.

Rachel spun around when she heard me laugh. "Oh ... my ... God!" she yelled. "You look like a horse with a feed bag."

Eric grinned and a few Cheerios flew from his mouth and hit the pavement. "I would give anything for a glass of milk to wash these down."

Two hours later we were at the start of the access road that would take us to Impact Lake – and the old training base. The van and the trailer were still where we saw them yesterday.

"I guess they're still out there somewhere," Eric said, kicking the trailer tire.

"*And* still searching for something," I added.

"They better not take all the meteorites," he joked. "Hope they save some for me."

We fought our way down the old roadbed – scrambling around trees and other obstacles. Rachel was a good sport and she never complained, not even when her front tire slipped into a crack and she got thrown from her bike. We were all riding pretty slowly so she didn't break any bones, but her right elbow had an ugly scratch from the spill. She wiped away the tiny stones that were stuck to her skin and got back on her bike.

At the washout, where the road disappeared, we took a mid-morning break. Rachel washed her elbow in the stream and when it dried I put the last three band-aids on it from the first aid kit in my pack. The wallet-sized first aid kit had been one of the supplies Rudi got for us in Egypt. I'd left it in my bag for an emergency, but I never thought I'd need to use it so soon.

Rachel and I each ate a banana – Eric said he didn't want one – and then we carried on up the washout and down the road. We hid our bikes in the same place as the day before and continued on foot until we got close to camp.

"You know," I said, stopping at the first major intersection of trails. "If those divers weren't at the camp yesterday, they're probably not going to be there now."

"What are you suggesting?" Rachel asked.

"Well, we could save a lot of time by *not* going to the base – not right away, anyway. And instead we could work our way along the north shore of the lake."

Eric nodded. "Good point. We know if we go straight, we'll find the camp. But if we take this trail," he pointed to a path going east, "it should follow the waterfront of the lake. Those guys had a lot of diving equipment with them and sooner or later they're going to want to use it in the lake."

I looked at Rachel. "And when we find their campsite, we'll stay back and spy on them. We should be able to figure out what they're up to just by observing them for a while." I took out my folding jackknife and walked over to a thick poplar tree. I hastily carved an arrow into the trunk, pointing in the direction we were traveling. I knew there were a lot of trails zigzagging through the area and I didn't want to get lost on our way back.

We walked for another twenty minutes and then we saw the lake. Eric took two quick steps, anxious to get to the granite outcrop that sloped down toward the water. But Rachel grabbed his wrist and stopped him. "What?" he said.

"I thought we didn't want to be seen," Rachel whispered. "We want to see what those divers are up to *without* getting caught – by anyone."

"Oh, yeah," Eric said. "I keep forgetting we're trying to be stealthy."

We stayed back in the tree line that formed a perimeter along the stony shore. Hidden there, in the shadows of the spruce and pine trees, we carefully examined the lake and waterfront as far as we could see.

Rachel looked at the shimmering water. "It would be nice just to put my hand in – feel how cold it is."

"Trust me," I said, pulling my binoculars from

my backpack, "it's freezing." I searched the water for boats or people, but didn't see anyone. "Impact Lake is deep and super cold. I wouldn't want to swim in here until late August – if even then."

Eric pointed to the west. "That's the floatplane base over there."

Rachel pushed a spruce bough away from her face and squinted at the shoreline about half a mile away. "Neat," she said. "Is that black thing the pier? The one from the old photograph?"

I nodded. "If we still feel like breaking the law later on, we can show you around the place." We didn't have much time to relax, but we still sat down under some trees and took a quick break. The rocks in front of us would have been a great place to fish from the shore. The water looked dark and deep and free of pesky weeds that always threatened to snag and steal hooks.

Rachel had offered to make sandwiches the night before and she now handed Eric and me each a peanut butter and jam sandwich. I could tell from the weight of it that it was going to be much better than the sandwiches my mom made. Rachel had spread a generous quarter-inch of peanut butter on one half, which bonded beautifully with a thick layer of raspberry jam on the other half. Eric finished his sandwich before Rachel even had hers unwrapped.

We left the rock and continued east along the trail around the lake. For the most part, the water remained visible on our right, but occasionally the path cut back into the forest to avoid a swampy area or to bypass boulders and other obstacles. We approached each bend in the trail cautiously – listening quietly for voices and campsite sounds. The last thing we wanted was to walk smack into the divers' camp. We needed to be sneaky.

After hiking for an hour in silence, I was ready for another rest. I had been following Eric, with Rachel making up the rear, when Eric's fist shot out – the Boy Scout hand signal for *freeze and be quiet*.

I stopped dead in my tracks, making Rachel bump into me. I spun around and put my fingers to my lips. *Shhh*.

All three of us stood frozen on the trail, listening intently.

After several minutes passed, I whispered, "Did you hear something?"

Eric nodded. "Definitely."

"What was it?" Rachel asked, wide-eyed.

"Not sure," Eric said, excitement still in his voice. "I think there might be something around the next corner. It could be people, but it might also just be a deer or rabbit. Hard to say."

We listened and watched for another minute.

"Let's get off the trail," I suggested, "and follow directly along the lakeshore for a bit. If they set up camp around here, we can approach it from the south. We're far from the base now, so no one walking around there will be able to see us."

Eric waited for me to carve an arrow into a tree and then he veered off the path and took us to the waterline. We continued moving east – always searching inland for the divers or –

"Hey," Eric said suddenly, "is that a boat?"

I looked around Eric. Up ahead, on a gravelly beach, was a small overturned fishing boat. It was made of aluminum, about the size of a rowboat, and it must have been there for years. Moss and other small plants were actually growing on the bottom, suggesting that the boat hadn't been used in a while.

"Neat," Rachel said, "it looks like someone forgot about it."

"Or died," Eric said, giving the boat a tap with his running shoe.

Rachel took a step back and looked around. "Huh."

Eric laughed. "I don't mean they died right *here*. I mean some old guy, who liked fishing here, might have died in the city. And maybe his relatives didn't even know this boat existed."

"*Or*," I said, "it leaks like crazy and no one wants to get it fixed."

Rachel examined the back of the boat, where an outboard motor might have hung decades ago. She bent over, wiped the grime away, and said, "It doesn't have a name."

Eric snickered. "It's an old fishing boat, Rachel.

It's not a cruise ship."

"I know *that*, smarty pants." She stood up and readjusted the straps on her backpack. "But sometimes people name a boat just for fun."

I nodded. "That's true. Mr. Jelfs has a boat kinda like this one behind his garage. And he has *Stinky* painted on it." I'd never seen him use it, but I always wondered why he'd call it that.

We left the boat-with-no-name and headed back into the forest. I took the lead and found the trail around the lake almost immediately – it was right behind the gravel beach. And *that* was where we encountered every hiker's worst nightmare.

Rachel grabbed my backpack, stopping me dead in my tracks. Up ahead, a big black bear was working his – or her, I suppose – way toward us, eating the wild strawberries that grew along the trail.

The noise Eric had heard earlier made sense now. The bear hadn't seen us yet, but he was heading right for us. In about a minute he would be sniffing our feet with his huge muzzle. My legs seemed glued to the ground, but I knew we had to do something.

I turned my head and as quietly as I could, I said, "Back up ... slowly."

We each took several paces backward.

SNAP!

Eric or Rachel must have stepped on a fallen branch. *Nuts!*

The bear's shaggy head shot up – his alert ears

listened for signs of danger like tiny satellite dishes. Seconds passed by and I thought he was going to go back to eating. But then his beady eyes settled on me and I knew for certain we were in big trouble.

Now what, I thought.

The what-to-do advice we had always heard about bear encounters was never the same. Sometimes we were told to curl up into a ball and play dead, while other experts said to climb a tree or to yell and make lots of noise. In our case, I didn't think he'd be fooled by us lying down on the ground. That would only make it easier for the bear to get his snack – three tasty kids. And would yelling really discourage an animal as large as a bear? I sure doubted it. I briefly considered climbing a tree, but there was no way all three of us could scramble up a tree fast enough to outrun the bear. So forget that.

The bear took a few cautious steps forward.

I matched him with three even more cautious steps backward.

Think, Cody. You have to do something.

The bear snorted, sending a wave of goose bumps up my arms.

I took a few more steps backward, never taking my eyes off the approaching bear. I didn't dare turn around to see where my friends were, but I sensed they were retreating too.

Maybe we could use the boat to escape, I thought. But there was no way we could drag it to the water *and* launch it successfully without being mauled first.

The bear waved his enormous head back and forth menacingly.

"Cody, the boat," Rachel whispered. "We could use the boat."

"I don't think we have time," I said quietly. "Plus, it might not even float."

"No!" she said. "I mean, we could hide *under* it – it's metal. We might be safe there."

I took another step back. "Good thinking." There were no other options available to us. We had to seek shelter somewhere and the old boat was our best bet.

"Just keep walking backward," I said, "slowly. If he starts to run ... then we'll turn and –"

"RUN!" Rachel screamed. "RUN!"

The last thing I saw before I spun around was the bear charging toward us. Eric was already out of sight. Rachel was three paces ahead of me, tearing back to the boat. We both broke onto the beach to find Eric struggling to lift one side of the vessel.

Panting from exertion, Rachel and I grabbed the edge of the boat on either side of Eric. We wrestled and strained to raise it, but the stupid thing would barely budge. Weeds and small trees had latched onto the boat over the years and we fought against them to rip the side free. Suddenly the boat became a lot lighter and we were able to lift it enough to get beneath it.

"Quick, Rachel," I ordered. "Get under!"

She dove in the gap between the front of the boat and the first row of seats.

At the same time I heard the bear crashing through the undergrowth behind me.

"Go! Go! Go!" Eric screamed.

I tried to wedge myself in the rear of the boat, but forgot I was wearing the bulky backpack. It got caught on the gunwale, leaving me half under the boat and half exposed.

"Hurry," Eric cried, "he's getting closer!"

I scrambled to free my bag and get back under the boat. I rolled onto my back and used my legs to keep the boat raised so that Eric could join us. "I got it," I bellowed. "Get under!"

I saw the bear storming toward us as Eric fell to his knees and rolled under the mid-section of the boat. When Eric was safely under, I bent my knees and let the weight of the boat seal us in.

SLAM!

The bear thumped onto the boat a second later. The boat shuddered violently but stayed put.

"Man, was that close!" I heard Eric say in the dark. His voice echoed eerily under our aluminum shelter.

I groped in the dark for my flashlight and flicked it on. "Is everyone okay?" I asked, waving the beam around.

Rachel said, "Yeah," but her voice was pretty shaky.

"I think I have to pee," Eric said, "but I'm all right."

Through the gaps under the boat's seats, I could see Eric and Rachel clearly. The deeper shape of the bow gave Rachel a lot more room at her end. She was leaning on one elbow, but she had enough space to crawl on her knees. Eric and I, on the other hand, were wedged in pretty tightly.

Outside we heard the bear snorting and grunting in frustration.

BAM!

The bear slammed a giant paw on the boat. I looked above me at the ceiling – which was actually the floor of the boat – and saw a dinner-plate-sized dent appear.

BAM ... BAM ... BAM!

The noise under the aluminum was deafening.

"Leave us alone!" Rachel yelled. "Go away!"

For a minute, I thought that would work. But then, without warning, the entire boat shifted a few inches. Light spilled from outside and I caught a flash of black fur – lots of black fur.

"Oh, no!" Eric said. "He's trying to do what he saw us do. He's trying to flip the boat!"

CHAPTER 6

I twisted my light and looked at the ground where the boat rested against the gravel. Four giant black claws appeared by my head, near the boat railing.

"Hurry!" I barked. "Climb onto the bottom of the seats. We need to weigh the boat down so he can't flip us." I was pretty sure he could upright the boat on its own, but with the added weight of three people pinning it down, we stood a chance.

Rachel had the most room to maneuver and she was the first to announce, "I'm in."

The back of the boat – my end of the boat – suddenly rose in the air half a foot before thumping to the ground again. The bear growled, unsure how to open his giant tin can of tasty humans.

"Faster, you guys!" Rachel yelled. "He's getting better at it!"

Frantically, I twisted and turned to wedge myself in the space between the bottom of the rear seat and floor of the boat. I had almost succeeded when the boat shuddered violently, knocking me to the ground.

"I'm in too," Eric said.

I kicked and wriggled my way back into the void. Finally, after countless scratches and bumps, I was in too.

But the bear didn't give up. We could hear his rear legs dig into the beach gravel as he prepared for another attempt to flip the boat. Sure enough, our metal shelter lifted, hung in the air for several seconds, and then crunched to the ground.

"Grab your packs!" Rachel yelled. "The more weight, the better."

I looked between Eric's folded legs and saw that Rachel was hugging her backpack close to her body.

"Hang on," I cried, "he's going to try again."

The boat shifted a bit, but the bear still wasn't able to lift us. *Thank goodness.*

"Yes," Eric hissed. "We're too heavy for him now."

"Or," I said, "maybe he's getting tired. Or bored."

We listened in our stifling shelter for the bear's next move. I hoped his next move would be to leave us alone and go away, but that was probably wishful thinking – he seemed determined. The minutes passed by and the sun continued to beat down viciously on the metal above us. Sweat dripped mercilessly from every pore in my body. I was too cramped to wipe my forehead, so I had to suffer and let the sweat sting my eyes. And the stress of hearing nothing except my racing heart was getting to me – I felt like I was about to scream uncontrollably.

"Hey, Rachel," Eric's voice cut through the silence. "Pass me a water bottle."

"Shhh! He'll hear you and come back."

"Just pass me something to drink," he whispered.

"I thought you had to pee," I said.

"I did before, but now I'm just thirsty."

I shone the beam of my Maglite at Rachel's backpack. She fumbled with the snaps and passed two bottles to Eric. He kept one and gave me the other. It was easy to open the bottle, but it was difficult to tilt the bottle up to drink. The floor of the boat was that close to our heads. I watched as Eric leaned out of his cramped upside-down seat and took a drink. I copied him and had a few swallows of water. We were all sweating like crazy and we had to stay hydrated.

"How much longer should we wait," Rachel asked, "before we take a look?"

I glanced at the luminous dial of my wristwatch. "Let's give it another fifteen minutes."

But after ten minutes, when we heard no sound outside the boat, Eric said, "I think he might be gone."

"Should we take a peek?" I asked.

"Might as well," he said. "We can't stay under here forever."

As quietly as possible, we rolled off the seats and stretched our limbs as best we could to get the blood flowing again. I felt like moaning with pleasure, but knew I had to keep silent. We decided that Eric would use his feet to elevate the side, while I looked around.

"Ready?" Eric whispered.

"Okay," I said. "Do it."

Eric lay on his back and used his feet to lift the

boat. The aluminum groaned in protest as he struggled to raise the vessel a few inches. I had my face pressed to the ground, ready to survey the beach. I squinted at the harsh sunlight and let my eyes adjust to all the sudden light. I didn't see any black fur.

So far so good, I thought.

"Higher," I whispered.

Eric raised the boat enough for me to stick my whole head out. I looked to the left and then the right. No bear.

"I think he's gone," I said.

"Look on the other side of the boat," Rachel suggested.

"Go a bit higher," I said to Eric.

He raised the boat a few more inches. I wormed my way out and snuck a peek over the top of the keel.

RATS!

The bear was still there! I flopped to the ground, scurried under the boat, and screamed, "Drop it, drop it now, Eric!"

No one needed to be told what to do next. Like well-trained soldiers we scrambled back to our battle stations – ready to weigh down the boat again. Next we heard the crunch of the bear's giant paws against the rocks.

"AHHH!" I screamed. "He's digging his way in!"

The bear pawed at the gravel outside the boat, shoveling stones away to make an opening. As the hole grew, he tried to wedge his face under the side. First, I saw only his muzzle, then a minute later half his head appeared – breathing stinky bear-breath into our already stinky coffin. It wouldn't take long now before he had us.

Suddenly, there was a loud smack against the gravel outside. It sounded like someone slapped a hockey stick against the beach. That was followed by a surprised grunt from the bear.

Whack!

We heard the noise again, followed by a voice. "Get away from there," a man ordered. "Beat it, Pluto! Let them be!"

The bear stopped digging and seemed to retreat.

Our rescuer rapped on the aluminum boat above us. "You can come out now," the stranger said.

The three of us didn't move. I shone the flashlight beam across the aluminum above us, so that we could see each other without being blinded. We didn't say anything, but I'm sure we were all wondering if leaving our shelter was the best thing to do.

"Hey," the voice said again. "It's okay. The bear won't be troubling you anymore."

"Are you sure?" Rachel yelled.

"Yeah," Eric hollered. "Are you certain he's dead?"

"Dead?" the man repeated. "No, Pluto's not dead. He's right behind me, under a tree, eating marshmallows."

The man's fingers appeared in the hole that the

bear – I mean, Pluto – had dug beside my head. He tried to lift the boat, but succeeded only in raising it an inch. He groaned loudly and dropped the vessel. We rolled out from our battle stations – from under the seats that were weighing the boat down. Eric and I used our backs to help the man lift the boat. When the boat was balanced high enough for him to handle the weight alone, we crawled out and stretched.

The stranger dropped the boat again.

"Holy smokes!" Eric screamed. "The bear's right there." Eric pointed past the man to a huge pine tree. Sure enough, the beast was relaxing on his bum and munching a bunch of marshmallows.

The stranger laughed and bent over to pick up a long, well-worn walking stick. When he straightened up again, my friends and I had a good look at him. Let me start by saying he was old – really old. He had to be at least eighty or ninety. His voice had made him sound young, but he looked even older than my Grandpa Arnold.

"Gosh," the man said, "you kids look pretty messed up."

I glanced at Eric and Rachel. The old guy wasn't kidding. We were covered with dirt and leaves and sweat. Rachel's neat ponytail looked more like a mop now – hair everywhere.

"What do you expect?" Eric shot back. "We almost got eaten by that thing." He pointed at Pluto for the second time. Pluto must have felt guilty, because he looked up at us and then back down at his big feet.

The old man scratched his weathered cheek with the walking stick. "Pluto wouldn't hurt a fly, son."

"Well, he was trying pretty hard to get to us," Rachel said. I noticed she was shaking as if she was cold, even though it was a million degrees out.

"Pluto can't eat anything except berries and marshmallows," the man said, defending his furry black friend. "Most of his teeth are gone, and the few he has left are so rotten he can't bear – no pun intended – to even close his mouth."

"If Pluto wasn't going to kill us," I said, "why was he attacking us?"

The old guy shook his head and laughed again. "He wasn't *attacking* you. He was trying to say 'Hello' – to get to know you. Pluto's curious, not dangerous – that's the way he's been since he was a cub. You savvy?"

"Huh?" Eric said. "I *what*?"

"You understand?" the man asked.

Eric nodded. "Pluto's claws sure look deadly."

The stranger took off a faded green baseball cap and pushed back the few gray hairs left on his head. He reset the cap and said, "Why don't we go over there and I'll introduce you proper. Pluto likes kids."

"Yeah," Eric said, "with marshmallows for dessert."

The man waved us toward Pluto with his

walking stick. Eric reluctantly followed, but Rachel shook her head and sat down on top of the boat. I was curious about Pluto, but decided to stay back with Rachel. I felt a bit bad for getting her involved in all this Impact Lake stuff and it didn't seem right to leave her alone when she was still upset.

When the old man was out of earshot, Rachel whispered, "Do you think that's him – the mad trapper?" She had stopped shaking and seemed to be calming down.

"I never thought about it," I said, "but, yeah, I suppose it could be him."

Rachel found her water bottle and drank half of it. "He sure doesn't look like a trapper, though."

I studied the man a bit more. He wore a camouflage T-shirt and brown safari shorts with lots of pockets. He had sandals on his feet – no socks. And he carried an army surplus rucksack slung over one shoulder. "No," I said, "he might be crazy, but he doesn't look anything like a trapper."

I sat down beside Rachel and we both watched Eric pat Pluto's giant head awkwardly. The old guy tugged and pulled on Pluto's floppy ears, encouraging Eric to do the same. Pluto threw his head back and moaned, showing his appreciation for the rough head massage.

Rachel pulled out her camera and snapped a few pictures of Eric playing with the giant black bear. "Without a picture for proof," she said, "no one will believe this."

Five minutes later, Pluto got bored, rolled lazily back onto his legs, and disappeared into the forest. Eric returned to the boat with the old man.

"My name's Jerome," the old guy said, sitting down on the boat. He took a long drink from his water bottle, lifted his cap again, and wiped his sweaty forehead. Playing with Pluto seemed to really drain him.

We told him our names and thanked him for showing up when he did.

"Yeah, that was pretty good timing," Eric said, "even if you say Pluto wasn't going to hurt us. Did you just happen to be out for a hike?"

"I followed your signs," Jerome said.

"You mean our tracks?" I asked. Maybe he *was* the trapper.

Jerome shook his head. "No, I mean your signs. You left arrows all over the bloody place, showing me where you were going."

"And you noticed them?" Eric asked.

"Look," he said, "if I went to the street where you live and spray painted big red arrows on all the houses, wouldn't you notice them?"

Eric shook his head. "Yeah, but –"

"– Well, it's the same thing," Jerome cut Eric off. "This is like my backyard. I'd be a fool not to notice those arrows you made. You savvy?"

"Yeah, okay," Eric said, "I savvy."

"So, you live here," Rachel asked. "Here at Impact Lake?"

Jerome's green eyes sparkled. "I live here each summer – every summer."

"Doing what?" Eric asked. "Are you the mad trapper everyone's scared of?"

"Jeez, Eric," Rachel scolded. "He just rescued us and now you're asking him if he's crazy?"

Jerome laughed and poked the stones on the beach with his stick. "People *think* I'm the mad trapper, Eric, so they stay away from here. And that suits me just fine."

"Why's that?" I asked. "Why do you want people to stay away from the lake?"

"I don't," Jerome said. "I want people to stay away from the base."

I knew the base was a restricted zone, but I was curious why *Jerome* wanted people to stay away. I didn't want to be rude, though, by pressing him. Sure, I admit I was being suspicious, but it seemed to me there was more going on at Impact Lake than what we could see – a lot more.

Eric continued with his more direct line of questioning. "And was that you trying to scare us yesterday when we were at the old base?"

"The base is a restricted area," Jerome said, not answering the question. "You're not allowed to go there. You could get in big trouble."

"We didn't know," I lied. "And anyway, we were

only looking around."

That really got Jerome's attention. "Oh," he said, sitting up straight. "You were looking for something – something at the base?"

"Huh?" I shook my head and tried to clarify. "No, we were looking around the base, not looking for anything *at* the base."

He laughed awkwardly and appeared to relax again. "Come on then," Jerome said, using his walking stick to help him stand, "let's go to my place and get you kids cleaned up so you look presentable when you get back home."

"We can wash in the lake," I said, pointing at the water.

Jerome laughed. "You ever try cleaning anything in ice water – without soap?"

He was right, but we still hesitated.

Rachel grabbed Eric by the wrist and me by the hand and pulled us away from Jerome. "Please give us a minute to talk," she said to him.

"No problem," Jerome said, sitting down on the boat again.

When we were under the big pine tree – the tree where Pluto was relaxing a few minutes earlier – Rachel said, "What do you guys think? Should we go with him?"

"I'm not entirely sure if we can trust him," I said. "But your arm looks pretty messed up and I do think we should get it cleaned before it gets infected."

Rachel frowned at her filthy elbow.

"Remember," Eric said to his sister, "we trusted Bruno and Rudi in Egypt. And that turned out okay."

"Are you kidding!" Rachel said. "We all got sucked into a wormhole and nearly disappeared forever."

Eric chuckled. "Oh yeah, that's right. But they weren't bad guys and it *did* all turn out okay – that was my point."

"What if we go along with him for now," I suggested. "And if at any time we get nervous or suspicious, we'll just leave. He might know the outdoors better than us, but if we made a run for it, there's no way he'd be able to keep up."

Rachel was silent, still twisting her arm and studying the cut from different angles.

"Look," Eric said, "we all know we're not supposed to trust strangers, but I think we may need to break that rule. Jerome might even know something."

"I think he's right, Rachel," I said. "He may be able to provide more clues to whatever is happening at Impact Lake."

In the end, Rachel reluctantly agreed. So the three of us followed Jerome into the woods, to a cabin we'd never been to before.

CHAPTER 7

Jerome guided us back down the trail toward the base. When we neared the intersection where I'd carved our first arrow, he slipped behind a cluster of cedar trees. We followed him in single file down a trail that we never would have found on our own, even if we *had* been looking for it.

"It's a good thing my place is just up ahead," Jerome joked, "because I don't have any more marshmallows with me today. And we *don't* want to run into Pluto without marshmallows." He thought that was super funny and he laughed so hard he began coughing.

We followed him around a sharp bend to his place. Only it wasn't what any of us thought it would be. In fact, his "place" wasn't even a building or a cabin. It was some kind of concrete bunker. Above the ground, we saw an array of solar panels – but nothing else.

"No way!" Eric said. "You live underground! That is *sooo* cool."

The concrete slab over Jerome's summer home was about twenty-four feet by twenty-four feet, but you really had to look to see where the forest began and where the house ended. He had disguised the concrete with natural stuff – sheets of moss, branches, stumps, etc.

"What was this place?" Rachel asked, looking around.

"When they built the floatplane base, it was a requirement that the base – actually, all bases – have a protective bunker for the storage of munitions. You savvy?"

"Yes," Rachel said, "that's bombs and stuff."

"That's right. They had to store the armaments in here, away from the barracks and the planes, for safety purposes. The lake is just over there."

We looked down his walking stick, to where he pointed through the trees.

He definitely could have been the one watching us yesterday, I thought to myself.

Jerome bent and lifted a latch – a latch I wouldn't have noticed in a hundred years. "They never did much bombing practice round here, but they had the bunker."

"And you made *this* your summer home?" I asked.

"No, not at first," he said. "I had a cabin on the other side of the lake, but a fire took it in seventy-six. I didn't feel like rebuilding, so I fixed up the bunker instead. She'll never burn down." Jerome laughed again, flicked a light switch, and walked down a metal stairway.

At first, we didn't follow him. Rachel, Eric, and I just stood there looking at each other. Jerome must have sensed our reluctance because he stopped halfway down and turned around.

"You told us you lived in a cabin. This isn't a cabin, it's a bunker," Eric said. Like me, he was wondering if we were walking into a trap.

"Yes," Jerome agreed, "a munitions bunker. I just told you that."

Eric shook his head. "What I'm saying is, how are we supposed to escape from down there *when* ... I mean, *if* you try to kill us?"

I winced at Eric's bluntness, but Jerome didn't seem bothered at all. "Well, it's up to you if you don't want to go in," Jerome said, squinting up at us.

Curiosity got the best of Eric again. "Okay. But if we come down there, you have to keep the hatch open in case we have to bolt." He was the first to follow the old man down the stairs.

"Hey," Eric said as soon as he got to the bottom of the steps. "*This* is the mad trapper's cabin? This is awesome!"

I stood on the floor of the bunker and looked around. Eric was right. The place *was* awesome. If Eric and I had discovered the bunker, we couldn't have fixed it up any better. The concrete room was well lit with lots of lights – solar powered, I supposed – and the bare concrete was painted bright white. He had his bed in one corner, a table and kitchen area in another, and lots of books and maps.

Even Rachel was impressed. "This is amazing," she

said. "It doesn't even feel like we're underground."

Jerome beamed. "I think my windows help." He pointed at the two giant posters on the wall. One was a photo of a forest scene and the other was of a lake – maybe even Impact Lake. The posters had real curtains hanging on each end.

"Cool!" Eric said, pointing at another wall. "You even have a flat screen TV."

"Well of course I do," Jerome said. "How am I supposed to watch movies without a TV?"

"I didn't think hermits watched movies at all," I said.

"What makes you think I'm a hermit?"

"Because you live all alone at a remote lake," Rachel said.

Jerome laughed. "But if I had ten neighbors living in cabins around the lake, then what? I'd just be a regular cottager, I guess?"

We were all quiet for a minute, considering what he'd said. He was right. We shouldn't have assumed he was a crazy hermit, just because there weren't other people around. Maybe he just liked living by the lake.

Eric continued to admire the TV while I wandered away to examine the book titles that lined the shelves. I took a few steps closer to get a better look at a leather-bound journal, but Jerome intercepted me. "Why don't we get you youngsters fixed up and then we'll talk some more?"

He pointed to a small sink in the corner and told us to clean up. We washed our faces with warm water and lots of soap, and Rachel did her best to clean her bashed up elbow under the faucet. After she dabbed it dry, I re-bandaged it using the supplies in the first aid kit Jerome handed me.

"That ought to do," he said.

"How come you showed us your place, if you want it to be a secret?" Eric asked.

"It's not really a secret." Jerome washed his hands and dried them on a towel. "It only looks like it's a secret because it's underground. Anyone can come and visit me, if they want to."

That didn't sound entirely believable, so I thought I'd test him. "So you don't mind if we tell people about this place."

"I'd rather you didn't, Cody," he said. "This is my home – for the summers, anyway. And I don't want people breaking into my home out of curiosity. You kids can understand that, right?"

We all nodded, even though I didn't entirely understand. Jerome said he wasn't a hermit, but he wanted people to stay off the base and he didn't want others to know where he lived. Something didn't make sense.

"And let's just keep your encounter with Pluto and me a secret. Savvy?"

"Why?" Rachel asked. "You said Pluto is harmless."

Jerome sat down at his kitchen table. "If you tell people what happened, they'll think Pluto is dangerous. But Pluto is harmless – he just needs to be left alone to live out his last years in peace."

We were all sitting around his little table, not saying anything. I thought about what he'd said and it sort of made sense. Had we immediately returned to Sultana after our bear encounter, we probably would have told the amazing story to our parents. We were off restricted base property when we found the boat, so we wouldn't have gotten in trouble. My mom and dad would have called the resource officers and reported that an aggressive bear was on the prowl at Impact Lake. And the resource officers would have caught Pluto and put him down – the polite term for killing him. Now that we were clean and calm again, I saw things from the old guy's point of view.

Jerome continued. "Think of it as a 'you scratch my back, I'll scratch your back' agreement. I helped you with your Pluto problem and I won't tell the authorities you were on restricted base property yesterday. And this way, you'll protect the base from more attention – from vandals – and you'll help Pluto too."

Eric twisted his head and gave me a goofy smirk. I knew he was about to say something that *he* thought was clever. *This should be interesting,* I thought.

"Well," Eric said to Jerome, "The thing about my

back is ... it's connected to my memory."

"What?" Rachel said. "That makes no sense."

I shook my head.

"Pardon me." Jerome looked confused.

"We'll keep quiet about you and the bear," Eric said, "if *you* tell us what you're *really* doing here. You savvy?"

I thought the old guy was going to yell at Eric for being so lippy, but he just laughed. "All right," Jerome said, "but then *you* have to tell me what you're really doing here too. Agreed?"

We all nodded.

"I'm the base trapper," Jerome said, "– the mouse catcher. I have eighty-seven mousetraps that I check each day, all summer long. That's my job."

"Oh, I get it," Rachel said. "So you really are a trapper, but not for big animals, just rodents."

"Yup." Jerome nodded, pleased with Rachel's ability to savvy – I mean, understand. "Years ago someone spread a rumor that I – a mad trapper – had a trap line at Impact Lake. What the rumor didn't say was that it was for mice. But that suited me fine."

"And that's what you do here?" I asked. "*All* summer?"

Jerome nodded. "That's *all* I do."

"And in the winter?" Eric said. "Where do you go then?"

"I have another cabin in the desert," Jerome said.

"In the desert?" Rachel repeated.

"In the southern states – New Mexico, to be exact."

"What do you trap there?" I asked.

"Nothing." Jerome said. "I wander around the canyons and mesas, looking for dinosaur fossils."

"Cool!" Eric said. "I'd love to see those fossils."

"If you're ever in New Mexico and can *find* my cabin," Jerome winked at Rachel, suggesting we'd never find his cabin, "I'll show you the fossils."

"Why don't you stay here?" I asked.

"Are you kidding?" Jerome laughed. "Why would I want to live underground, next to a frozen lake, during a Canadian winter? I'm an old man – I can't take the cold anymore."

"What are you retired from?" Eric asked. "What was your job before –"

"– But enough about me," Jerome said, cutting Eric off. "Why don't you tell me why you came here – *two* days in a row?"

I told him our story, ending with, "So we were curious what those divers were really diving for. *And* why they lied to us about the type of plane they were looking for. But we couldn't find them anywhere."

Jerome's eyes widened. "What do you mean, you 'couldn't find them'?" His voice took on a nervous edge.

Eric and I looked at each other.

"We searched all over the base," Eric said, "but they were nowhere."

Jerome lifted his hat, ran his palm over his head,

and set the cap back down. He paced in a small circle next to the table. "Okay," he said suddenly, "we better get you kids on your way."

He led us outside and back down his secret trail. When we neared the point where the paths intersected, he made us wait so that he could creep forward and examine the area first.

"He sure got paranoid once we told him about those divers," Eric whispered. I nodded.

Jerome came back to walk us out to the main trail. Before saying good-bye, he reminded us of our promise. "Please don't tell anyone about Pluto." We watched him slip back into the forest, toward his bunker.

"There's no way he's *just* a mouse catcher," Eric said. He asked Rachel to turn around and then unzipped the main pocket of her backpack. Eric dug around in the bag she was still wearing. "Yesss! Pepperoni sticks. You're my favorite sister." He pulled out a small plastic bag and opened it.

When Rachel heard her pack being closed again she turned around. "He sure had a lot of books on geology and rocks and minerals." She accepted a pepperoni stick and chewed on it thoughtfully. "Did you see them all, Cody?"

I nodded, and at the same time tried my best to remember the words printed on the old journal I'd seen. The thought vanished as quickly as it came. I shook my head. *Oh, well*, I thought. It was probably nothing important and I'd probably recall it later, anyway. That's the way my brain worked.

"Nuts!" Eric said suddenly. "I really wanted to ask him if he knew about that old machine in that hidden, off-limits hangar. He'd know what it was for." Eric looked at Rachel and grinned. "You savvy?"

Rachel groaned. "Don't tell me you're going to be saying that all the time now."

We laughed and began our trek back to our bikes. It was four-thirty in the afternoon and there was no time for us to do any more hunting for our mystery divers. And even though Jerome gave us a few marshmallows, we *really* didn't want to bump into Pluto again.

By the time we got back to Sultana, we were pretty exhausted. I don't think it was the ride to Impact Lake and back, as much as the stress of our encounter with the giant bear. Before I said good-bye to Eric and Rachel, we all agreed not to tell anyone about Jerome or his furry friend, Pluto. A promise was a promise.

When I informed my mom that I hadn't had supper yet, she quickly made me a grilled cheese sandwich. And while I was debriefing her about our "fishing trip" – leaving out the Pluto and Jerome parts, of course – Dad walked in.

"How was your trip to Impact Lake?" He poured us both a glass of milk and sat down across from me.

I swallowed a mouthful. "Good," I said.

"And you stayed away from the restricted area around the base, right?"

I looked at my sandwich and nodded. Mom must have told him we were going fishing at Impact Lake. I hoped he wasn't suspicious.

"How many did you get?" he said.

I stared at my dad, not sure what he was asking. My mind began racing. *Mosquito bites, comic books, flat tires – what was he talking about?* I opened my mouth and then closed it again.

My dad sighed like he always did when he thought I wasn't paying attention. "*Fish*, Cody. Did you and your friends catch any *fish*?"

"Oh, yeah. Right." I laughed nervously. "I mean, no, we didn't catch any."

"That's too bad. It would be nice to have some fresh lake trout."

I continued lying in a feeble attempt to make my big lie sound believable, if you know what I mean. "Well," I went on, "Eric had a couple of bites – one even bent the line pretty good – but they both got away. And Rachel ... Rachel umm ... she caught one too. She reeled it in all the way to the shore. But then it slipped off the hook just as we were about to land it."

Dad nodded, accepting my shaky summary. "Was anyone else around the lake?"

"No," I said, perhaps a bit too quickly. "It's pretty quiet there."

"Hmm." My dad seemed kind of disappointed. "So you didn't bump into Mr. Whiting?"

"No ... who?"

"Mr. Whiting," Dad said again. "The trapper – Jerome Whiting."

I dropped my sandwich and stared at my dad. I'm sure my mouth was wide open. "How ... how do you know about him?"

"Two or three times each summer Mr. Whiting picks up supplies from the gas station. He seems like a nice old guy." Dad laughed. "Whenever I ask him how the fishing is at Impact Lake, he winks and says 'Terrible.' And then he tells me to spread the word. He's friendly, but he doesn't like people around the base. Just as well – it is restricted."

"Hmmm," I said, still at a loss for words.

"Well, don't blab about him all over town," Dad said. "Things are pretty slow and I don't want to lose the old guy's business."

"And that's his last name – Whiting?" I asked.

Dad guzzled his milk and put down the glass. "Yup, and he's not even a trapper. He's a retired geologist – just like his dad. That's what he told me, anyway."

Mom went outside to weed her flower beds and Dad headed off to sharpen the lawnmower blade in the garage – leaving me to my thoughts. My sandwich *had* tasted terrific, until my dad began talking, that is. I considered what he had said as I finished off my late supper. And I was still chewing when I turned on the computer.

I found the website on Impact Lake – the one we were looking at the day before – and clicked on the group photograph from 1940. I stared at the kid in the front row with his dog, Mickey. *Could that boy be Jerome Whiting?* I wondered. If the base commander, Major Reginald Whiting, had a son, he could certainly be the boy in the picture. I mean, if the little guy in the photo grew up, he would be around Jerome's age.

I looked over at the dog. *An Andalusian*, it said. I quickly looked up "Andalusian" in the dictionary. *No way!*

A breed of mouse-hunting dog.

Could that be a coincidence too? Or was the boy – the owner of Mickey, the mouse-hunting dog – Jerome, the mousetrapper of Impact Lake? But if that was true, and he was hanging out at the base since 1940, why wouldn't he tell us that? What was Jerome hiding? Or, was he after the same thing the divers were after – whatever that was?

I went back and looked at his dad, Major Reginald Whiting. Major Whiting's eyes certainly looked similar to Jerome's, but maybe my brain was just trying to make everything fit together. I wasn't getting anywhere staring at the old photo so I decided to try a different approach.

I did a search for "Geologist Reginald Whiting."

His military career seemed to begin and end at Impact Lake. But I thought it might be helpful to know what he was up to before the war. I found lots of online military biographies on the major, which only repeated what I already knew about his days at Impact Lake.

I was about to turn off the computer, when I spotted something different – *PAPERS AND LECTURES BY REGINALD WHITING 1936-1939.* I clicked the link and the screen filled with all the boring geology studies and papers the guy was involved with before the war. My finger floated over the BACK button, ready to leave the site.

Whoa! I stopped and stared at the title of a report near the bottom of the page: *DIAMOND-BEARING KIMBERLITE DEPOSITS OF IMPACT LAKE MANITOBA.* I double-clicked the title and began to read the scanned pages of a report that the major wrote back in 1938.

Even though I had only read the summary, the hairs on the back of my neck began to stand up.

CHAPTER 8

"Hello?" Rachel answered the phone.

"Rachel, wake up Eric," I said. "Right now! We have to go back to Impact Lake."

"Why?" she asked, excitement building in her voice. "What's going on?"

"I think I may have found something – something interesting. I was on the computer last night ... and ... well, I'll tell you about it in half an hour. Just see if you can wake up Eric." It was half past seven in the morning. By the time I had finished reading the old geology report last night, it was too late to call Eric and Rachel. But I had set my alarm so that we could get an early start.

Thirty minutes later I was tearing down Eric and Rachel's driveway. Rachel greeted me at the door. "Mom's at work. Come in."

I followed Rachel into the kitchen and sat down across from Eric. He was finishing a bowl of cereal.

"Perfect," he said, grinning into the bowl.

"What is?" Rachel asked. She sat down too.

"I love it," Eric said, "when I get the right ratio of milk to cereal. I don't like having a lot of milk left over in the bowl. *Or* having to add more milk to my cereal. This is a great way to start my day."

"Whatever." Rachel shook her head at her brother.

"*Anyway*," I said, "I think I may have found something interesting last night."

Eric pushed his bowl away. "Let's hear it."

"Diamonds!" I said.

"Huh?" said Eric.

"I think everything has to do with diamonds – not sunken airplanes or gold or meteorites, but diamonds."

Rachel's eyes grew big. "What did you find?"

"Way back in 1938 – when the major was just a geologist – he did a study on Impact Lake."

"Okay, I'm with you so far," Eric said.

Rachel reached over and punched her brother on the arm. "Shhh! Stop being silly."

"– And in his report he claimed that there used to be a diamond-bearing type of rock – called kimberlite – just north of Impact Lake. And –"

"Hold it!" Eric cut me off. "So diamonds are found in a rock called kimberlite?"

I nodded.

"But the major said the kimberlite was gone?" Eric said. "Sooo ..."

"Let him finish the story. Gosh, you're annoying in the morning." Rachel paused. "Correction – you're annoying all the time!"

Eric only grinned in reply.

I continued. "I guess this kimberlite stuff forms

giant carrot-shaped pipes in the earth, and the Major believed that one used to stick out of the ground near the lake. The kimberlite's not there now because the glaciers came along twenty or thirty thousand years ago and scoured and scraped and gouged the kimberlite away."

"Sooo ..." Eric said again, "if it's gone, why'd you wake me up?" He reached for the cereal box.

"Here's the good part," I said. "The major found that most of that kimberlite – the rock that contains the diamonds – got scraped and collected into a natural low area behind the base."

Eric dropped the cereal box and stared at me.

"Yes," I said, reading his mind. "That gravel pit behind the mystery hangar is full of diamonds – it's all kimberlite! That's what his report says anyway."

Eric closed his mouth and tried to swallow.

"And remember that weird machine in the hangar?" I said. "I think they used *that* to get the diamonds out of the gravel."

"Diamonds," Eric said, trying out the word. "Not planes. Not meteorites. Not illegal mouse fur."

"Diamonds," Rachel murmured, "I never would have guessed."

"I wonder why no one built a diamond mine there," Eric said.

I shrugged. "Maybe no one read his study. Maybe people thought he was nuts. Maybe everyone got busy with war stuff. Who knows?"

"And that's why the Major demanded his float-plane training base be built at Impact Lake," Eric said, "so that he could go after the diamonds – the diamonds he suspected were right there?"

"Yup," I said, "and he probably did it all with Air Force money."

Eric smiled, appreciating the major's sneakiness. "I guess that explains why the base was ... conundrum and –"

"– Controversial," Rachel corrected.

Eric frowned at his sister but went on. "And why it had people talking about what was going on there."

"You really have done your homework." Rachel smiled at me.

"I have one more little theory."

"What's that?" Eric asked.

"Major Reginald Whiting?" I paused.

Eric and Rachel both nodded.

"I think he's Jerome's dad. And I think Jerome knows something about the diamonds and that's why he's acting all suspicious."

I explained what I had found, ending with the leather-bound journal in Jerome's bunker. I had only seen the book for a second, and it was upside down, but I was absolutely certain now that the embossed letters on the front spelled *MAJOR R. WHITING*.

Rachel's head bobbed up and down. "It does seem like way too much of a coincidence," she said.

"That the boy in the photo has a mouse-hunting dog called Mickey and that Jerome's still at the base, after all these years – *and* still hunting mice."

Eric frowned. "But why would he spend every summer, for his whole life, hanging out at Impact Lake?"

"Exactly!" I said. "Why is he really at the base?"

"Maybe he's looking for the diamonds," Rachel said.

"Could be," I said.

"Or maybe he's in some kind of trouble," Rachel said. "In which case we should try and help him out –"

"Hold it! Hold it! Hold it!" Eric said. "I don't mind going to the base again to look for diamonds and meteorites and airplanes, but why do you think he needs our help? He seems like a guy who can take care of himself."

I shook my head. "Rachel's right. Those divers are after something out there. And didn't you see the look on Jerome's face when we told him about them? He looked really scared. Maybe he found the diamonds years ago and now he's guarding them – guarding them from the divers."

Eric still wasn't convinced.

So I tried again. "It doesn't hurt to check. We go to Impact Lake one more time and we make sure their van and trailer are gone. If they're still there, we go to the base and hike around the lake the other way. Their camp has to be somewhere on the south side."

"Look," Rachel said to her brother, "Jerome saved us from that big black bear and we owe him. I know he *said* Pluto was harmless, but I think he only told us that so we wouldn't freak out and go into shock. Let's face it, if Jerome hadn't come along when he did, we'd still be hiding under that old boat. And you," she pointed at Eric, "would probably be starving to death."

Eric laughed. "All right, all right. But my bum's still sore from yesterday's ride."

I grinned at my friend. "Don't worry about that. I think I may have found us a free ride, but we have to hurry."

We scrambled to fill our packs with food and drinks – Rachel even found a bag of marshmallows – and twenty minutes later we were outside the service station. Eric re-inflated his tire while I told them my plan.

Earlier that morning I had seen Mr. Jelfs put his chain saw and toolbox in the back of his truck. I suspected he was going to cut firewood near Betula Lake – that's about five miles past Impact Lake – but I asked him just to make sure.

"As soon as I have breakfast and gas up," he had said, "I'll be on my way."

"Dad said he hasn't shown up yet," I said to Rachel and Eric. "But as soon as he does, we'll ask him for a lift."

After ten minutes went by without anyone showing up, I began to worry he had changed his mind, but then he rolled up to the pumps with his ancient farm truck.

"Hey, Mr. Jelfs," I said. "Can we catch a ride with you as far as the Impact Lake trail?"

"Impact Lake is off limits," he said. "You kids got no business there."

"Only the base is restricted," Eric reminded him. "We'll be at the other end of the lake."

He squinted at the three of us and then studied our bikes. "Something wrong with your wheels?"

Eric shook his head. "We just need to be there by eleven and we're running out of time."

"Okay," he said. "But you have to all ride in the back. Inga isn't going to move for anyone."

We looked inside the truck cab and saw Mr. Jelfs's shaggy dog sitting on the passenger seat. She had her head way out the window, anticipating a fun, breezy ride to the forest.

"And remember," Mr. Jelfs said, lifting Rachel's bike into the back, "this box has a lift like a dump truck. So if you kids don't behave, I'll flick a switch and tip all three of you onto the highway."

"If you don't feel like flicking that switch, just hit a bump in the road. We'll fall right through all the rust in this wreck," I teased.

"It's not a wreck," he shot back, "it's an original 1947 Dodge – a classic. And antique automobiles are supposed to look like this. Now climb in before I change my mind."

"That was great timing, Cody," Rachel said, repairing her ponytail. The wind in the back of the truck had whipped her hair all over the place. She fixed it in no time at all, transforming it from disheveled back to sheveled – if *sheveled* is even a word, that is.

"Yeah." I turned around and waved goodbye to Mr. Jelfs and Inga. "I figured we'd have a lot more time to go exploring if we caught a ride here."

"It would be awesome if he drove by later," Eric said. "I got a feeling we could be in for a long day." He indicated the van and trailer with his chin.

We strapped on our packs, swallowed some water, and set off down the trail to the old floatplane base. After two trips to Impact Lake, we felt pretty comfortable on the abandoned road and we made good time. We only stopped to stash our bikes off the trail. From there we hiked the rest of the way.

At the first fork in the road we all stopped.

"Okay," I said. "If we keep going straight, we know we'll find the base, the lake, and the trail we were on yesterday. I think this path swings around behind all the buildings and goes along the south shore. Should we give it a try?"

Eric knelt down next to some dents in the earth. He touched the tracks of an off-road vehicle with his fingertips, like he'd seen the professional trackers do on TV. "Hmm." Eric pretended he was deep in thought and then he stated the obvious. "I believe someone in an ATV headed off in that direction – perhaps recently."

I laughed.

"Duh!" Rachel shook her head and led the way. "I think you had too much sugar this morning."

Eric chuckled and followed us through the forest.

I was convinced that the ATV tracks we were following were those of the researcher and the divers. This had to be the route they took, the route we missed two days ago. Then after thirty minutes – just as I was having doubts again – I finally saw Impact Lake sparkling through the trees. I was happy to see the water and happy to know that after three days we were finally getting our bearings.

We snuck quietly to the waterfront and looked around. We knew better than to expose ourselves on the open rocks along the shore, and instead stayed hidden among the trees. Off to the left – maybe half a mile away – we saw the mess hall and the long pier that stretched out over the water. It was good to know we were exactly where we wanted to be. *No complications so far*, I thought.

Rachel took out a pair of binoculars and surveyed the lake. "I don't see any people, or any fishing boats," she said. "Hey ... but I *can* see that old boat we hid under yesterday. It's straight across, on the other side." She kept her finger pointed at the spot, while Eric and I took turns trying to see it with the field glasses.

"Cool," I said, passing Eric the binoculars.

"I hope Pluto stays on that side of the lake," Eric said.

We had lunch on a giant slab of granite next to the main trail, with the lake shimmering through the trees. It would have been a nice picnic, except Eric complained the whole time about the food Rachel had packed. Carrot sticks, apples, celery, and granola bars weren't my idea of a terrific meal either, but I wasn't going to complain.

"Can't I just eat the marshmallows we brought?" Eric whined.

"Go ahead," Rachel said. "Cody and I can run faster than you."

"So?" Eric said, grabbing the marshmallows. "What does *that* have to do with anything?"

"It means that when we all start running from the bear – because we *don't* have any snacks to distract him – he'll catch *you* first and eat you. And Cody and I will escape."

Eric crammed Pluto's treats into his bag and reluctantly ate some carrots while Rachel and I laughed.

Eric suddenly hissed. "SHHH!"

I was about to tease him for not having a sense of humor, when he did it again. "SHHH! Listen!"

Rachel and I froze.

I heard it now too – the crunch of something on the trail, followed by the sound of leaves being stepped on. *Yikes!* A chill went up my spine. *This time we had nowhere to hide.*

"Quick, Eric!" Rachel ordered. "Be ready with the marshmallows."

The noise on the trail became louder – whatever it was would be coming around the corner any second.

Eric reopened his backpack, pulled out the marshmallows, and grabbed a handful. He stretched out his hand and said, "Ready."

The crunching noise moved even closer.

Catching us all off-guard, the lady from the gas station walked around the corner and right into our picnic. We sat there, mouths open, not sure what to do or say.

She stopped in front of Eric and looked down at the marshmallows in his outstretched hands. "Why thank you," she said, bending over and grabbing a couple. "Is it okay if I take two? I love these things."

CHAPTER 9

"Hey," she said, sitting down to join us, "didn't I meet you boys at the gas station?" She popped a marshmallow in her mouth and then she looked back and forth between the three of us, waiting for someone to say something. I think we were all relieved she wasn't a bear, but still surprised to see her strolling around the lake.

I finally managed to nod and began telling her who we were.

"Well it's fantastic to meet you – Rachel ... Eric ... Cody." She repeated each of our names and smiled. "I'm Kelly by the way. I thought we were the only ones out here, so it's nice to see some friendly faces."

Eric didn't waste any time getting to the heart of the matter. "So," he began, "you're here to check out the base to see if it should become a Historic Site?"

Kelly nodded. "Yeah. How did you know that?"

"My dad works at the service station where you got gas," I said. "He told us."

Kelly nodded. "Ahh, small towns," she said. "Word gets out quick."

"Did those divers find the planes they were searching for?" Eric asked.

Kelly threw back her head and laughed. "They

might find them, if they ever decided to get wet."

"What do you mean?" Rachel asked.

"Well," Kelly said, "this is our third day here, and they never went for a single dive yet. When I ask them about it, they keep telling me they have to do more research."

"Research?" I said. "What are they researching?"

"Oh, who knows?" she said. "So far, they spent most of their time walking the trails and lurking around the base. But to tell you the truth, I don't care what they do. I have my own work to finish."

"What are you working on?" Rachel asked.

"It's not that interesting. I was hired by the government – the Department of National Defense, to be specific – to visit the base here and catalog all the buildings and equipment that are left on the site."

"You're right," Eric said, "that sounds a bit boring."

Kelly laughed again. She seemed like a happy person. "That's what I said – at first. But it's pretty important work."

"Why's that?" I said.

"Because the government is about to make a big decision," Kelly said. "They're going to either dismantle the entire base or preserve everything and turn it into a National Historic Site. But they wanted someone – that's me – to take a final look around to see if the place is worth preserving forever."

"Is it?" Rachel asked. "Is it worth preserving?"

Kelly shrugged. "I don't know yet."

I looked at my friends, who stared silently back at me. The base could be turned into a park so that everyone could come see all the amazing history – or it could be destroyed.

Kelly seemed to mistake our silence for disinterest. "But aside from my evaluation," she added, "the base is still pretty mysterious."

"What do you mean?" I said.

"There was some weird stuff going on here during the war – really weird stuff. And the more I poke around in the records, the stranger it gets."

"There are records?" Rachel asked.

"Sure," Kelly said, "lots of them. In fact, many of the camp ledgers, log books, and purchasing records are still in boxes right here on the base. If the site becomes protected, all those documents will be scanned and put into a digital archive. There's a lot of history at this base. In fact, I'm heading over to the quartermaster's office now. You're all welcome to join me if you'd like."

Rachel looked at Eric and me. "You know," she said, "I could go with Kelly and see if there's anything *interesting* in the archives." Rachel placed a lot of emphasis on the word "interesting" and gave us a hard stare. "You guys can go ahead without me."

Kelly must have thought we were reluctant to look through dusty old papers. "It's okay," she said, "if you'd rather continue on your hike. But if you spot Greg and Vincent, stay out of their way."

"Who?" Eric asked.

"Oh, sorry." Kelly said. "Greg and Vincent are the divers. Greg's the big guy and Vincent is the shorter guy. They're brothers. Anyway, they said they'd be diving this morning. If you follow the quad trail for another half mile, you should see our camp and the ATVs."

"Why do we have to stay out of their way?" I asked.

"They're really protective of all their new diving gear," Kelly said. "Big Greg nearly went off on me yesterday when I tried to help him move his scuba tanks." The memory made her shudder.

Eric and I nodded. We both remembered how jumpy they got when we tried to examine the stuff on the trailer.

"We can meet back here at four o'clock," Eric suggested.

"Terrific," Kelly said, standing up. "You boys have fun."

I needed to confirm what my dad had told us at the gas station two days ago. "So," I said, pretending I didn't know anything at all, "are Greg and Vincent helping you with your research?"

"No way." She seemed shocked at the notion. "The *only* reason they're here with me is because the government paired us together to save money. The brothers got some sort of permit to dive for artifacts related to the old base. Someone thought it would be better if we pooled our resources, but no, we are not a team."

Rachel and Kelly straightened their packs and headed off down the lake-front trail, toward the base. From behind, they looked like they could be sisters. Kelly was a bit taller than Rachel, but they both had the same color hair and the same practical ponytail bouncing on their backs.

"She doesn't have to worry about us getting in their way," Eric said when the girls were out of sight. "I'm not going anywhere near Greg and Vincent. Not if I can help it, anyway."

"No kidding." I stood up and put on my backpack. "Kelly seems like an okay person, but I still don't trust those divers one bit – *if* they're even divers."

"Let's just stick to the original plan," Eric said. "We find their camp and spy on them."

We headed off down the path in the direction Kelly came from. We set a brisk pace and covered the half-mile in only twenty minutes.

Eric froze suddenly. He crouched down and pointed up ahead.

I squinted through the trees.

"There," Eric said. "Under the big pine tree. Two tents."

I scanned the trail ahead of us but saw nothing. Then, suddenly, I saw them too. The bright orange and yellow colors of the nylon tents gleamed in the sunlight.

Eric whispered in my ear. "Let's go into the forest and sneak up on their camp from the south."

I nodded and followed Eric off the trail into the woods.

Fifteen minutes later, Eric stopped again. Their campsite was about one hundred feet ahead. The two small tents were thirty feet or so apart. One tent was a bit smaller than the other, but it was tight and level. The bigger tent looked like it was erected by a drunken person in the middle of the night. Half the lines were loose or not fastened at all and a quarter of the tent had collapsed. Our Boy Scout leader would have made us do it over.

"I think they're gone," I said. "Both ATVs are missing."

Eric agreed, but we still spent fifteen minutes hiding behind a wall of junipers – listening and watching. A circle of rocks made up a campfire pit and beyond that sat the trailer belonging to one of the off-road vehicles. The scuba tanks and dive gear were lined up on the ground next to the trailer. The cool water of Impact Lake lined the north side of their camp, three hundred feet away. A stand of thick cedars had prevented us from seeing their camp from the other side of the lake.

"I suppose," Eric said, "if they took both ATVs we should be able to hear them coming from a long way off."

"Yeah." I knew where he was going with this, but

the thought made me nervous.

"Well, let's check everything out – while they're gone. Maybe we can find some clues or maps or something."

I nodded. "Anything that will help us figure out what they're *really* doing here."

Eric stood up, took off his backpack, and walked into their camp. Three coolers were stacked up behind the larger tent and Eric headed straight for those.

"What are you doing?" I whispered.

Eric was in the process of lifting a white plastic lid off a blue cooler box. "Huh?" He stopped.

"Why are you looking at their food?" I said. "Who cares what they've been eating?"

Eric lowered the lid again. "I thought maybe I could borrow some chips or cookies or ... you know, if they had lots of extra ..."

I shook my head and went over to the big tent. I opened the flap and peeked inside. There were two messy sleeping bags and clothes strewn about, but nothing useful or interesting. I felt a bit guilty doing it, but I decided I might as well look in Kelly's tent too. She was a much tidier person. Her sleeping bag was lined up perfectly on a pink foam pad and she had one corner folded back – ready for her to climb into it. Another backpack – I suppose with her clothes in it – was next to her sleeping bag.

Eric walked over to the scuba gear and gave one

of the upright tanks a kick.

BANG!

The scuba tank tipped over, rolled against a rock, and then separated into two pieces. Eric and I stood frozen, looking down at the scuba tank – a *fake* scuba tank.

"Holy smokes!" Eric said. "It's plastic. It's not steel or aluminum."

I bent over and picked up the top of the tank. "It's light as feather." I held the top with the phony valves. "These are just props."

Eric took the piece and examined it. "No wonder they wouldn't let us near their stuff. Anyone who touches this would know it's not a real scuba tank right away."

"That must be why they grouched out on Kelly," I said. "She would have accidentally discovered they weren't real divers."

Eric and I looked inside the hollow tube of the fake scuba tank.

"What is it?" I said, watching Eric slowly extract something from the core.

"I'm ... not ... sure." He pulled out large, crazy-looking goggles with lots of straps.

"Whoa!" I said. "I think those are night vision goggles."

"Why would divers need these?" Eric said.

"Whatever those guys are," I said, "they're *definitely* not divers."

Eric looked deeper inside the cylinder and found another pair of goggles. And under the special glasses were walkie-talkies. "I've got an idea," Eric said.

"I bet I know. You want to steal their gear right?"

"No." My friend giggled. "Let's switch every-thing on, so that all their batteries die. That way, *if* they turn nasty, they can't use this stuff against us."

"That's brilliant."

We quickly turned on all their gadgets and recapped the tank with the phony cover. The other two scuba tanks were just as fake as the first. Inside we found duct tape, lots of rope, and even several boxes marked "motion sensors" – it was all bizarre.

"These guys are starting to give me the willies," I said.

"It's almost like they're hunting something," Eric murmured, "or trying to catch something."

"Or someone," I said. "When my dad goes hunting, he never takes stuff like this. He puts on a bright orange vest, grabs a rifle, and off he goes. I can't think of any logical reason for them to sneak around with all this hidden spy gear."

"No kidding," Eric mumbled.

"Maybe I was totally wrong," I said, "thinking this had anything to do with diamonds. Maybe the original meteorite –"

"– Shhh!" Eric cut me off. "Someone's coming!"

I listened to the sounds of the forest while Eric replaced the last cover. I was straining so hard to hear the motorized growl of their ATVs, I almost missed the crunch of feet shuffling down the trail toward us.

We looked around the camp to make sure we didn't leave any signs that we'd been there. I nodded at Eric and raced back to our backpacks and our juniper cover.

"Just ... in ... time," I said, gasping for air. "There they are!" Five seconds after we dropped to the ground, the divers popped into the small clearing next to the lake.

"Man, was *that* close!"

Big Greg emerged from the trail, followed by Jerome – Vincent made up the rear. At first, they looked like three buddies coming back from a mid-day hike around the lake. That is, until I noticed Jerome had his hands bound behind his back.

"Holy smokes!" Eric whispered. "They captured Jerome."

I nodded and watched them parade the old man to the campfire area. They instructed Jerome to sit down on a lawn chair. Vincent rummaged through the fake cylinders until he found the duct tape. He didn't notice their electronic equipment was on. *Thank goodness.* Greg roughly held Jerome's arms while Vincent taped his wrists to the chair.

"This is bad," I mumbled. "Really, really bad."

"We need to get help," Eric whispered, "right away."

I totally agreed with Eric, but neither one of us made a move to go. We both wanted to see if there was some way we could help Jerome now.

We watched Greg take two wetsuits from a giant equipment bag and carry them to the lake. He jumped on a rock that was partly submerged and began wetting the scuba suits that would have kept him warm, had he been a diver. It took him a minute to get them both soaked because they kept bobbing up. When they were saturated he dragged the now-heavy suits back to camp and hung them on a sturdy rope that Vincent had strung between two trees.

"These guys are sneaky," I said, peeking between the branches. "They must want Kelly to think they really were diving today."

"That's actually a relief," Eric said. "At least we know Rachel's safe with Kelly and that we can trust her. If they're trying to fool her, she can't be one of the bad guys."

"Yeah, and that's good because we're *definitely* going to need Kelly's help on this one." I looked over at Eric who had a strange frown on his face. "What's wrong?" I asked.

"I wonder why they brought him here?" Eric said. "They know Kelly could come along any minute and then they'd be busted."

Eric had a good point. "This must only be a temporary stop on the way to wherever they're taking him," I whispered. "We better follow them to see where they're taking him, *before* we go for help."

"Jerome looks pretty scared," Eric said. "Maybe we should let him see us, so that he knows he's not alone."

I nodded. I'd hate for him to give up hope, thinking no one was around to help him.

We decided that I would try and sneak up closer to the camp, straight across from the direction Jerome was facing. My beige shorts, green T-shirt, and darker complexion allowed me to blend into the forest a bit more than Eric's blue shorts, yellow T-shirt, and paler skin did. Okay, I was able to blend in *a lot* more than Eric was.

While Greg and Vincent messed about, trying to make it look like they had been diving, I snuck around the camp and approached from the west. I had to really concentrate on keeping an eye on both men, while staying quiet at the same time. When I knew where both guys were, I would quickly crawl closer. But each time I lost sight of them, I froze and became scared to make a move. I really didn't want to end up taped to a lawn chair.

Finally, I felt I was within range of Jerome's sight line, yet far enough away that I wouldn't be seen behind the birch clump that screened me. I waited patiently for the right opportunity to reveal myself. At last, both Greg and Vincent disappeared behind the tents.

I jumped out and waved my arms around, trying

frantically to get Jerome's attention. But his head was down and his chin was resting on his chest. *Jeepers, was he sleeping?* I desperately wanted to scream his name, but forced myself to keep quiet. I was forty feet from the guy and he wouldn't look up.

I dove behind the tree again and caught my breath. *Now what was I supposed to do?* I looked around the birch tree. Vincent was leaning four diving fins against a tree, and Greg was consulting a map that he pulled out of his back pocket. When Vincent finished, he sauntered over to his partner and studied the paper with him. They had their backs to me.

Looking around, I spotted some pine cones under a nearby jack pine. I crawled over and collected a handful of fresh cones. The guys were still examining the map, so I took a pine cone and threw it at Jerome. It landed in the soft ashes of the fire pit and made a tiny puff, but Jerome didn't hear or see it.

I took the heaviest cone and threw it again – even harder.

THUMP!

It popped Jerome right on the head and bounced off to the left. That got his attention. He looked up and saw me waving my arms around. He blinked a few times and then opened his mouth to say something, but I quickly put my fingers to my lips. I mimed *SHHH* and his mouth snapped shut again. I pointed to where Eric was hiding to let him know

I wasn't alone.

He sat up straight and gave me a wink. I think our presence really did give him a spark of hope. *You scratch my back, I'll scratch yours,* I thought. He had saved us from Pluto, now we'd return the favor – hopefully.

Greg began folding the map, so I ducked behind the tree again. I heard them moving around near Jerome, so I knew I had to wait to make my getaway. Every time I snuck a look around the trees, one of them was facing in my direction. Lucky for me, Jerome saw my predicament.

"Hey!" Jerome yelled.

The sound of his voice startled everyone – including me.

"Where are you taking me?" he yelled. "What do you want?"

Greg and Vincent stopped what they were doing and walked around to face him. This was my chance – they were finally looking away.

"You know exactly what we want," Big Greg said calmly. "And we want it today."

"I have no idea what you want, son," Jerome said. "So you better at least give me a hint."

"We want your daddy's diamonds."

CHAPTER 10

I knew I was supposed to make my escape, but I stayed glued to the ground. I had figured that diamonds were somehow involved in the history of the old floatplane base, and now that my suspicions were confirmed, I wanted to know everything – all the details.

"And," Greg was saying, "if you don't tell us where the diamonds are ... well, let's just say, I hope you can hold your breath underwater for a long time."

"Like forever," Vincent added, just in case Jerome didn't get the message.

"Look, old man," Greg said, "it'll be a lot easier if you tell us where the major stashed the diamonds. We know they're around here somewhere and ..."

"Okay, okay," Jerome said. "I'll take you to them. They're at the base. But I need to eat something first. I can't even stand. I'm too weak right now to walk there. You savvy?"

I'm not sure if he was acting or not, but it was smart of Jerome to give us a head start so that we could get to the base before Greg and Vincent. I waited for the bad guys to go look for food and then I made my escape.

"Did you catch all that?" I asked Eric when I met

up with him again.

"Yeah, every word." He scrambled to put on his backpack. "So they *are* after the diamonds Major Whiting recovered during the war. You were right."

I grabbed my bag and followed Eric into the forest. Ten minutes later we were on the main trail, hustling back to the floatplane base. We had to get there and find Kelly and Rachel *before* Greg and Vincent showed up. I was sure Jerome would eat slowly and stall them for as long as he could, but I didn't think he would be able to buy us more than one hour before they'd show up at the base.

Eric stopped to have some water when we got to the spot where we separated from the girls. "How did those guys know about the diamonds?" Eric said.

I shrugged. "Well, it's not a secret. It's just that no one read the major's old geology reports, or no one who read them cared. So everything was actually hidden in plain sight, as they say."

"Hmm," said Eric. "I wouldn't have thought those guys were the type to read lengthy field reports – reports from *before* the war."

"Yeah, that's true. They don't seem particularly bright, but I suppose they could have done the research and figured it all out. Heck, that's what we did – and we did it all by accident."

"Hmm," Eric repeated.

After another twenty minutes of brisk walking,

the buildings of the Impact Lake Floatplane Training Station No. 451 spread out in front of us.

We were both sweating and panting lightly – it was hot.

"Where should we begin looking for them?" I asked.

Eric wiped his forehead with his wrist. "Kelly mentioned something about a Quarterpounder or Quarterback or Quarter something –"

"That's right!" I snapped my fingers. "She said they were going to check out the quartermaster's office. He's the guy who would have ordered everything for the camp. His office might be attached to – or be close to – a supply warehouse."

We urgently headed for one of the bigger buildings, always keeping our eyes peeled for signs that the girls were nearby. Eric opened the door to the shop and yelled as loudly as he dared, "Kelly! Rachel!"

No response.

We tried two more buildings without any luck. Eric and I were both soaked with sweat by the time we got to the main mess hall building at the center of the complex. I began to feel panicky, because we were running out of time. The bad guys would be here soon.

"There!" Eric said, pointing to a small building next to a garage. "An open door!"

The windows of the office were boarded up but

the door was propped open to allow sunlight in. Eric got to the doorway first. "Rachel?"

"Eric?" I heard Rachel's voice from inside the building. "Come in here. You should see what we found."

A second later I was inside the office with Eric and the girls. "Never mind that," I said, letting my eyes adjust to the dim light, "we've got serious trouble. The divers captured Jerome and they're coming here – here to the base."

Kelly was sitting behind an ancient metal desk and Rachel was on a wooden chair next to her. The table was covered with old documents.

Kelly jumped out of her seat first. "WHAT?"

"Don't joke around," Rachel said. "That's not even funny."

"We're not kidding," Eric said. "We were watching their camp and we saw the whole thing ... and we heard them too. The old guy's in trouble and we have to get help."

Kelly unzipped a side pocket on her backpack and pulled out a cell phone. She flipped it open and turned it on with a shaky hand. "Come on ... come on," she whispered. "SHOOT! Nothing – no signal at all." She snapped her phone shut and wedged it in her front pants pocket.

"We knew they were related!" Rachel said. "We just figured that out when you guys walked in."

"Huh?" I said.

"The quartermaster," Rachel said. "His name is Red Stevenson and his name is on everything here." She pointed at all the old order forms and ledgers.

"We know that name," I said. "We saw it on some requisition papers."

"But so what?" Eric said. "What does that have to do with anything? We have to find help."

Kelly took a deep breath. "Greg and Vincent's last name is *Stevenson*. They must be Red Stevenson's grandsons, or nephews, or something. Based on all the weird stuff Red Stevenson ordered for the camp, he must have been in cahoots with the Major."

"It all makes sense now," Rachel said quickly. "I told Kelly about your diamond theory and everything here proves it, Cody. The major couldn't have organized it all by himself. The quartermaster – and probably a few other people – were in on the diamond collecting scheme."

Kelly flicked off a powerful LED lantern that she had hanging from a nail in the rafters. "Red Stevenson must have blabbed to his grandsons about the diamond harvesting and now they want them."

I quickly repeated everything we saw and heard at Kelly's camp.

"You know," Kelly said, "I always had a feeling those guys weren't divers or researchers. They're too dumb to pitch a tent, never mind recover an airplane."

"Big Greg said he was going to throw Jerome in the lake," Eric said, wrapping up our report, "unless

145

he tells them where the diamonds are."

"Okay," Kelly said, "you three go for help and I'll go back to make sure your friend is safe."

I shook my head. "That won't work. It'll take way too long. Plus, if a car doesn't come along down the highway when we get there, it could take hours to get to Sultana and bring help back here."

"And no one would believe us anyway," Eric said, backing me up. "Everyone still remembers when we tricked the whole town last month with a fake Egyptian tablet. They'd think it was another prank."

"You did what?" Kelly looked very confused.

"We can explain that some other time," I said.

I turned to Rachel. "What if you take Kelly to the bikes and ride together back to the van? Then you can both drive directly to town and get help."

"What about you guys?" Kelly asked. "I can't leave you alone with those criminals."

"Don't worry about us," Eric said. "We can be pretty sneaky too. We can stall them, or do whatever we have to, until you return with the cops."

Kelly considered that plan. It was the only strategy that made sense, the only one that gave us enough time to save Jerome from the icy waters of Impact Lake.

"Okay," she said. "But please promise me you'll be careful. Those guys have crossed the line and they're getting desperate. Who knows what they might do if they catch you."

Kelly and Rachel decided to leave their bags in the quartermaster's office so that they could travel faster down the trails.

"Give Kelly my bike," I said to Rachel. "The seat is easier to adjust than Eric's and the tires are bigger."

Rachel put her backpack on the desk. "Okay," she said.

Kelly fished the keys for the van from a small side pocket on her rucksack and then tossed the bag next to Rachel's. She gave Eric and me a final nod, said "good luck," and followed Rachel outside.

I closed the door of the building behind me and watched them jog north to the old access road. When they were out of sight Eric turned to me. "Okay, so now what?"

I opened my mouth to answer him, but before I could say anything, he roughly pulled me around the corner.

"I think they're coming!" Eric whispered. "I thought I saw something behind you – between those other two buildings." He carefully pointed at some shacks about three hundred feet away.

We both crouched low and waited to see if the divers would emerge from one of the paths that wound around the base. Thirty seconds passed and then they appeared.

"Whew!" I said, ducking back out of sight. "That was close."

"I wonder where Jerome's going to take them?"

Eric shook his head. "I hope he has something to offer them," he said. "Because they're going to get fed up pretty quickly if he just leads them on a wild goose chase all afternoon."

I nodded. "Do you think he really knows where the diamonds are? I mean, if he did, why would he keep coming out here – for all those years?"

"Maybe he's been protecting his dad's diamond stash," Eric suggested. "Or maybe *he's* still looking for them –"

"– Or maybe he is a bit bonkers," I said. "I mean, he lives underground by himself, in a wartime bunker. That's not considered normal behavior by most people."

We watched as Jerome was taken through the base, wedged between Vincent and Greg. His hands were no longer tied, allowing his arms to swing freely at his sides. I wasn't positive, but it sure seemed like he was putting on a "feeble old man" act as he crawled down the path. When we followed him to his hideout the day before, he had walked slowly but with confidence – like a mountain goat on a cliff. But now he was staggering about as if his legs were made of rubber.

I chanced another look around the corner.

They were walking toward the main mess hall. I studied Jerome's face and noticed his eyes were scanning the area. He had to be searching for us – for help. Seconds before he vanished on the lakeside of the mess hall, we made eye contact. He kept his head straight, but his eyes looked to the side and directly at me, holding my gaze. He gave me the slightest of nods, acknowledging that he saw me, and kept walking. *Don't worry, Jerome, we savvy, and we'll get you out of this.*

"We need to hear what they say," I said. "Then maybe we can stay a step ahead of them."

We bolted across the rocky courtyard to the mess hall. Pressing our backs against the wall, we shimmied along the building toward the front. Then we hid under the main porch and listened to Vincent and Greg mumbling near the bottom of the steps.

"Go look for Kelly," Greg said to his brother. "She's around here somewhere doing her stupid research. When you find her, keep her busy until we get the rocks."

Vincent disappeared, leaving Jerome alone with Big Greg.

"So the major kept the diamonds in here?" Greg asked, poking Jerome in the kidney with two fingers.

The old guy pretended to look confused. "I ... I think this is the building he meant."

"And *what* does *that* mean? What did he say?"

Jerome spoke loud and clear, so that we could hear everything. "Dad liked to talk in riddles. Sometimes when I asked him if I could see the diamonds, he'd say, 'Sleep on it.' So I wondered if they might be under the floorboards in my old bedroom."

Greg looked frustrated. "And you're trying to tell me you never lifted those boards – after all those years? Give ... me ... a break!"

Jerome sounded perplexed. "I think I looked there back in sixty-four ... no, wait, it was sixty-six ... But I can't remember what I found there. You savvy?"

"What else did your pappy say about the diamonds? And unless you want to go for a swim, your memory better start clearing up. Do *you* savvy that, old man?"

Jerome seemed to ignore the threat. "Well, he did say two other things that you might find interesting. He used to say 'Diamonds are a dog's best friend.' And another time he told me that Mickey – that was my dog back then, Mickey – was living in the lap of luxury. I never knew what he meant, but I also never forgot it."

All Eric and I heard were the summer sounds of insects while Greg considered Jerome's clues.

Greg cleared his throat. "Did your mutt – I mean, Mickey – have a doghouse at the base?"

"Sure he did," Jerome said, "he's a dog. A dog has to sleep somewhere."

Greg sighed. I was pretty sure he was losing patience. "And *where* exactly was this doghouse?"

"It's near the latrines," Jerome said helpfully. "A latrine is a toilet and in the military they're called –"

"– I know what a bloody latrine is!" Greg

screamed.

"All right, all right ... don't blow a fuse, sonny. I'll take you there when we're done here." I heard the old guy climb a couple of steps. "Now I wonder which bedroom was mine ... Gosh, that was a long time ago ..."

When they were both inside the mess hall, I grabbed Eric's wrist and said, "Come on! I have an idea." I looked around to make sure Greg wasn't nearby and then sprinted into the forest to the north. I stopped when I felt we were safe.

"What's up?" Eric said.

"We're going to get those guys off Jerome's back, by giving them what they want – diamonds."

Eric grinned. "Go on."

"We're going to hide a bag of fake diamonds in Mickey's doghouse. We know Jerome is going to take Greg there next – that's what he was trying to tell us – so we need to beat them there."

"But how are we going to make diamonds?" Eric asked.

"Raw, uncut diamonds are ugly," I quickly explained. "They just look like little pieces of quartz or glass, and we know where there's lots and lots of glass."

I passed Eric my pocket knife and explained my plan. "Go to the hangar where we found that diamond separating contraption and cut a piece of that black leather from the counter under the window. Then head over to the garbage dump. I'll either meet you at the dump or on the trail back to the base. Hurry!"

Neither one of us wasted any more time talking. Eric took off for the old hangar and I raced for the road that would take me to the glass pile. Twice I blew a turn and had to backtrack. But finally I was at the ancient dump. I knelt down next to the largest section of smashed glass and began rooting through the rubble. The sweat poured into my eyes as I sorted the fragments. I avoided the bits made of clear glass and instead collected hazy, clouded pieces.

When I had about sixty pieces of glass that could pass as fake diamonds, I carefully looked them over again. A few had sharp edges – I know that because I cut my fingers – so I flicked them away. But the rest looked great. Each piece had lots of edges and a few even sparkled brilliantly when the sunlight hit just right. I kept them tight in my fist and began jogging back to the base. A noise up ahead suddenly startled me and I dove into the forest and hid behind a log.

Eric ran past me at full speed.

"HEY!" I shouted.

Eric skidded to a stop and turned around. A paper-sized piece of black leather was in his hands. I poured my glass diamonds into the middle of it.

"No way!" Eric said, poking at the glass. "They're absolutely perfect."

"We just need to get them to the doghouse before

those jerks show up."

Eric took a four-inch piece of scrap wire that he'd found in the hangar and twisted it tightly around the diamond pouch. We hightailed it back to the base and headed straight for the washroom building. I hadn't seen any doghouse on our first trip, but Eric insisted one was there.

When we had the latrine in sight, we paused behind a shed and examined the area for any signs of Greg or Vincent. Eric elbowed me and indicated the top of a small, metal-roofed doghouse with his chin. The structure was so encased in weeds and poplar trees it was amazing he'd seen it at all.

"Nuts!" I said. "Here they come!" We watched Greg push Jerome toward the washroom building. They were too far away to see Mickey's half-hidden shelter.

"Man!" Eric said. "And we were so close to stashing the diamonds. We only needed a few more minutes."

Suddenly Vincent appeared from around one of the warehouses and ran up to his brother. We couldn't make out what he was saying, but he looked pretty worked up. And whatever he said, it got Greg agitated too. Both men nervously looked at the buildings surrounding them.

"I think they figured out Kelly took off on them," Eric said.

"Yeah, that's it," I whispered. "Vincent probably

spotted the backpacks in the quartermaster's office and now they're wondering what it all means."

"It would sure be nice if Jerome could distract them for us ..."

Just then, Greg decided to point in the opposite direction, at one of the farthest buildings. Vincent turned his back to us too, leaving only Jerome facing our way. I leapt from my cover and waved my arms about frantically – again, desperately trying to get Jerome's attention.

This time Jerome savvied immediately.

When he nodded at me, I quickly held up five fingers. *Stall them for five minutes.*

Another nod from Jerome.

He turned and walked around Greg and Vincent. Greg mumbled something and I heard Jerome say, "I think Mickey's doghouse is on the other side of the latrines." He never waited for a response – he simply guided them away from us.

I took off my backpack and left it with Eric behind the shed. When the bad guys were out of sight, I sprinted to the doghouse. I took a nail that I'd found behind the shed from my pocket and pushed it into the soft wood inside the doghouse, just above the entrance. Without even looking, I hung the diamond pouch on the nail and raced back to Eric.

My heart was racing so fast I thought I was going to have a heart attack. I flopped onto the ground, closed my eyes, and tried to calm down.

"Here they come," Eric announced.

I was too exhausted to sit up, but I was happy Eric was letting me know what was going on.

"They're heading for the doghouse," he whispered. "Now they're walking around it ... checking it out."

I looked around the corner with Eric. Jerome stood back a few feet while his captors groped around the exterior of the small shelter. "Come on, you guys," I mumbled, "make an effort at least."

"Kelly was right," Eric said, "they really are kind of useless."

Greg's face turned bright red. He starting yelling at Jerome and kicked the doghouse in frustration.

"Hey!" Vincent yelled. He fell to his knees and stuck his head inside Mickey's house.

Greg stopped hurling threats at Jerome and waited for his brother to come out. Vincent stood up and proudly held up our bag of fake diamonds.

CHAPTER 11

"The nail must have fallen out when Greg kicked the walls," I said.

"Thank goodness," Eric said. "I think they would have been too lazy to look inside the doghouse."

Eric and I watched nervously as Greg untwisted the wire we had twisted only fifteen minutes earlier. We couldn't see the glass bits, but suddenly Vincent let out a "Yahoo!" that made both of us jump.

Eric slapped me on the back. "It worked, Cody. They think they're real!"

Jerome cautiously scanned the area for us. Greg and Vincent might be dumb enough to be fooled by dirty pieces of crushed glass, but I'm sure Jerome knew we had something to do with it.

Greg continued to stare at his treasure, poking the chips with his fingers. I was starting to worry that he was getting suspicious, but then I realized he was mesmerized by the diamonds – I mean, glass. Finally, he retied the bundle using Eric's wire and shoved the pouch deep inside the front pocket of his jeans.

"Congratulations," Jerome said. "That's tremendous – you guys found the diamonds. Dad would be pleased. I hope you both have a pleasant summer. No hard feelings." Jerome took a few slow steps backward.

But they weren't done with him yet.

"Not so fast, old man." Greg sprang at Jerome and wrapped a powerful hand around his wrist, preventing him from escaping.

"Hey!" Jerome yelled. "We had a deal. You got what you were after. Now let me go!" He wriggled for a few seconds, but gave up. There was no way he was going to win a fight or a footrace against Big Greg. "Why don't you leave me alone?"

Greg put his hands around Jerome's shoulders, like they were buddies. "Well, just think about it for a minute," Greg said calmly. "We can't have you telling people we kidnapped you. That just won't do. And, you know how it is – accidents happen."

"What's that supposed to mean?" Jerome asked.

Vincent piped up. "It means, you might have been fishing from the pier today, when you suddenly slipped into the lake and drowned."

"You won't get away with it," Jerome said. "That's murder!"

"No," Greg said, "that's called an *accidental drowning*. And it's *your* fault, not ours."

"Yeah." Vincent began snickering. "You should have learned how to swim."

Greg shoved Jerome in the direction of the dock. The old guy stumbled for a few steps, recovered, and then began walking away from us.

Eric's eyes looked as if they were going to pop

right out of his head. "Kelly and Rachel are *never* going to make it back in time with the cops. What are we going to do?"

"If only we had some kind of weapon," I mumbled. "Holy smokes! Look!" I pointed to the tree line, three hundred feet away.

"Oh, no," Eric said, "it's Pluto! We don't need another complication."

I grinned as an idea flashed through my mind. "I think that bear is going to help us rescue the old guy. Jerome scratched Pluto's back, now Pluto can return the favor."

"Are you serious?" Eric said, nervously watching the approaching black bear. "What can that fur ball do?"

I grabbed the marshmallow bag from Eric's backpack. "Stay here," I said. "I'm going to fetch Pluto."

"But then what? How's a bear going to stop them from drowning Jerome?"

I quickly explained my plan. "They have to pass by a bunch of the smaller buildings on the way to the pier, right?"

Eric nodded.

"Well, if I can time it just right, I think I can trick them into believing that a killer bear is after them. Hopefully, they'll dive for cover in the nearest building and stay there until Pluto is gone."

"And that's going to save Jerome?" Eric asked.

I shrugged. "I don't know. It might not work at all, but it's worth a try. We can't sit around doing nothing."

I left Eric with our packs and ran off to greet Pluto. We met behind one of the garages, out of sight from Greg and Vincent. The giant bear stopped twenty feet from me and tossed his head up and down. I hoped that was his way of saying, "Hey there, Cody, I remember you. You're okay and I won't kill you."

I threw a marshmallow in front of him and he quickly inhaled it, like a giant vacuum cleaner. I took ten steps backward and dropped another puffy white treat. "Come on, Pluto," I whispered, "faster. Pick up the pace."

The bear took a few more steps and ate the second marshmallow.

I turned, ran ten steps, stopped, and turned around again. Pluto was standing still, staring at me. *Jeepers, Pluto. Chase me already!* I walked back to the bear, showed him a third marshmallow and then ran again.

This time it worked. Pluto began loping after me and my marshmallows at medium speed, like we were playing a friendly game of tag. I rounded the corner of the garage and spotted Jerome and his captors in the distance. They were approaching the quartermaster's office and still heading for the lake. They never saw me, so I kept quiet as I jogged up behind them.

I glanced back to check that the bear was still hot on my heels. *Good boy!*

When Greg and Vincent were twenty feet from the building where we found Kelly and Rachel, I began screaming. "BEAR! KILLER BEAR! RUN AND HIDE!"

Greg and Vincent spun about and froze. I don't know if it was the shock of seeing a kid, or the surprise of seeing a huge bear chasing a kid, but the dummies just stood there.

"HIDE!" I kept yelling. "HE ATTACKED MY FRIEND! RUN INSIDE!"

They snapped out of it. Greg looked around briefly and then ran into the nearest building – the quartermaster's office. Vincent piled in behind his brother and slammed the door. And like the mean guys I suspected they were, they left a senior citizen and a thirteen-year-old kid outside with a six-hundred-pound killer black bear.

Perfect!

I ran up to the front door and dropped some marshmallows on the steps.

Pluto was so excited to get his sticky reward that he slammed his big head right into the bottom of the door. The door shuddered and I wondered what Greg and Vincent were thinking. Inside, I could hear desks and other furniture being piled against the door. The windows were boarded up from the outside, so the men inside had no idea what was really going on. *Serves them right!*

Eric ran up to us grinning.

Jerome gave each of us a hug and then put his fingers to his lips, signaling for us to keep quiet. "Ahhh ..." he began screaming like he was being mauled. "Get off ... me ... Ahhh ..." Jerome let his voice trail off in an eerie death wail.

Pluto looked at us like we were all bonkers. I tossed him a few more marshmallows and he groaned in appreciation.

Jerome waved us away from the front door so we could talk. "Thanks a lot, boys," he whispered. "If you hadn't shown up when you did, well – well, it wouldn't have been pretty. Hey, where's Rachel?" He looked around anxiously.

"My sister's all right," Eric said. "She went for help an hour ago."

"How long can Pluto keep them trapped?" I asked.

"Only for as long as he gets marshmallows," Jerome said. "Unfortunately, as soon as the sweets are gone, he'll get bored and wander off again."

"Then let's just dump the whole bag," I said, "and run for the highway."

"That won't work. Pluto will scarf them all down in ten seconds and leave." Jerome shook his head. "Plus, they have those off-road vehicles somewhere and they'll catch up with us pretty quickly. And to be honest, boys, I don't know if I have the energy to make a run for it."

"What about your hideout?" Eric asked. "We could hang out there until help arrives."

The old guy shook his head again. "That's where they found me this morning and that's the first place they'll look."

"So the only thing we can do is keep feeding Pluto," I said, "and hope that help shows up?"

"This is stupid!" Eric said. "We have to hide or run away or *something*."

Jerome nodded. "I agree. You boys have done more than enough. You should head for the highway and I'll stick around with the bear."

Gosh, old people were stubborn.

"We're not leaving without you," Eric whispered. "And we have to all leave while we can."

"No!" Jerome said defiantly. "If they escape, they may never be caught again. I don't want them lurking around Impact Lake anymore. I'll keep them cooped up until the cops come, and Pluto will help."

We all looked at Pluto. He was slouched with his back against the door – paws relaxed and resting on his furry belly.

Eric and I looked at each other. We didn't have to say anything – we knew we'd both be staying to help Jerome.

Jerome took a marshmallow, licked one end, and walked over to Pluto. He pressed the sticky marsh-mallow near the top of the door. Pluto rolled over and reached up to grab it. His long claws scraped the wooden door from top to bottom. The noise inside the small office must have been terrifying. Jerome winked at us and then yanked on Pluto's ear. The beast growled and groaned. We knew the bear was in heaven, but Greg and Vincent didn't.

Pluto sank down on the steps and waited for the next marshmallow.

Jerome returned to the neighboring building, where Eric and I were waiting. "Could you find my bunker again from here?" he asked Eric quietly.

Eric nodded. "What do you need?"

"Go as fast as you can and fetch all the marshmallows you can carry."

"No problem." Eric took off toward the northwest, leaving me alone with Jerome.

Pluto let out a loud growl and paced in a small circle in front of the makeshift jail.

"Oh no," Jerome said. "It looks like he's getting bored. You better toss him another one." He sat down on the front steps of the building and waited for me.

I copied what Jerome did earlier and sucked on one end of a marshmallow. I pressed Pluto's reward firmly against the sheet of plywood that covered the front window.

The bear knew what to do. He stood up, leaned his giant front paws against the wood, and scratched at the marshmallow. The marshmallow fell to earth, but not before the bear left a huge gouge in the window covering. Pluto ate the dirt-covered snack without complaining. He leaned his bulk against the door and licked his lips. He appeared to be enjoying the shade of the tiny veranda.

I walked over to Jerome and sat down next to him. *What a day!*

"How many you got left?" he asked.

I held up the clear plastic bag. "Maybe a dozen."

"That ought to hold us," Jerome said, "until Eric gets back."

I passed him one of our unopened water bottles and we both sat quietly for a few minutes. Pluto looked content grumbling to himself, so we made no move to fatten him with more marshmallows.

"How'd you boys fake the diamonds?" he asked.

I told him the story of how we found the camp and saw him being held prisoner, and then how we collected the smashed glass from the dump.

"Smart," he said. "You're sharp boys – really bright. I was hoping you might be able to help me stall them, but I didn't think you'd come up with that."

"But are there really diamonds here somewhere? Did your dad, Major Reginald Whiting, actually find diamonds?"

Jerome raised his eyebrows. "Oh! You know about my dad, do you?"

I explained what we'd figured out and what we'd discovered in the old hangar. "So that funny machine *is* for diamond mining?" I asked.

"Let's just back way up to 1935, Cody. And I'll tell you the *whole* story."

"Okay," I said, eager to hear what had happened all those years ago.

"My dad was a pretty smart geologist when he was younger – that was way before the war. He knew all about Impact Lake and the meteorite that smashed here thousands of years ago. That was common knowledge. But Dad had a theory that when meteorites slam into the earth they create diamonds. He thought the heat and pressure of that kind of impact would instantly make diamonds. You savvy?"

I nodded. *Yes, I savvy.*

Jerome continued. "Dad surveyed and studied and drilled in this area for five years, but never found a single meteorite or impact diamond." He paused and took a sip of water. "But here are two things that are interesting. First, years later, geologists discovered that Dad's theory was bang on. The impact of a meteorite can and does create super small diamonds – they're called *nanodiamonds*, by the way. So my father was right!"

"Hmm," I said. "What else?"

"Huh?"

"You said there were *two* interesting things. What's the second thing?"

"Right," Jerome said. "While my dad was investigating the area for these impact nanodiamonds, he found a massive deposit of kimberlite. You probably figured this out already, but kimberlite is the stone that contains diamonds. Dad believed that the advancing glaciers ground and scraped the kimberlite ..."

"I know," I said, "I read his paper ... *and* his theory."

"You read Dad's thesis?" Jerome looked impressed.

"Yes," I said. "That's what helped us figure most of this out. But the report I read never said anything about nanodiamonds. I would have remembered that."

"No, it wouldn't have mentioned the impact diamonds. Dad kept that a secret. He thought it was so farfetched no one would believe him."

"Okay," I said, "so what happened?"

"Dad became obsessed with diamonds after Mom died – that was back in 1939. He desperately wanted someone to believe him and to fund a mining operation at Impact Lake. But then World War Two started and no one felt like throwing money into a crazy project like a diamond mine – and in Canada, to boot."

"I guess I can understand that," I said.

Jerome continued. "Anyway, the Royal Canadian Air Force wanted to use my dad's experience in managing drilling camps and running the geology department at the university. So they asked him if he would accept a commission as a major and start a floatplane training base."

"And that's why he located it at Impact Lake?" I

asked. "So that he could secretly mine the kimberlite for diamonds?"

"Yes, but it's not what you think. Dad was an honest man – he was just stubborn. He wanted to prove to everyone that he was right – that there were diamonds in Canada."

Suddenly, Eric came around the corner and flopped down a pile of marshmallow bags. He saw that we were in the middle of a serious conversation, so he sat down quietly next to me

"But did he really find diamonds here – here in the kimberlite?" I asked.

Jerome shrugged. "I think he did ... but who knows. When Dad died, he wasn't rich. I believe that if he did find diamonds, he gave them to the military to support the war. That was the kind of man he was. He wasn't a criminal."

"Did he have any partners?" Eric asked. "Maybe they kept some of the diamonds and really did stash them here somewhere."

Eric and I looked around the base, imagining all the possible hiding places for diamonds.

"Sure," Jerome said, "that's possible. And that's why I used to spend my summers here looking for diamonds, and searching and searching and searching ..."

"Why'd you stop?" Eric asked.

Jerome laughed – kind of a sad, lonely laugh. "In the sixties and seventies, I'd leave my wife alone at home with the kids and I'd spend the summer out here looking for treasure – for those stupid diamonds. Then in the eighties I would lie and say I was fishing with my buddies, but I would *still* come to Impact Lake. And now? Now my wife is dead and I come here because it's beautiful and it's peaceful and I can think about how stupid I was and how lucky I was. You savvy?"

Eric and I both nodded.

"Wait a second," Eric said. "If you don't think there are diamonds hidden here *anymore*, why'd you get all freaked out when we told you about the divers?"

This time Jerome nodded. "Well … I started wondering if I had missed a clue over the years, or if someone knew something I didn't know, or … or who knows what? I know I sound like a paranoid old fool, but I was a bit scared they were looking for me."

"Why would you even think that?" I asked. "Has anyone ever come out here looking for you or the diamonds?"

He shook his head. "No, but I always worried that day would come. Years ago you had to go to a university library to read Dad's geology reports and his diamond studies. But now, with that Internet thing, you can sit in your house in Albuquerque and discover there are diamonds in Manitoba. And then there are all the military records. Dad had to order some pretty crazy stuff to keep his diamond operation going. I'm sure copies of those documents are somewhere in Ottawa or Winnipeg or ..."

Pluto grunted and rolled over onto his legs. Eric quickly responded and pressed half a bag of marshmallows into the doorframe. The bear scraped and clawed at the door, gobbling up the sugary snacks as he freed them. *If he wasn't diabetic, he soon would be*, I thought.

Eric came back and joined us on the steps. "What about that machine in the far hangar?" he asked quietly. "How does it work?"

"That thing was a ton of fun to watch – when it was working properly, that is. There's a big drum on it that they used to coat with beef tallow and –"

"Beef tallow," Eric repeated.

"Yes," Jerome said, "it's just fat – like lard, only a lot smellier. Anyway, we would put a thick coat of beef tallow on that drum and then pass a crushed gravel and water mixture over the grease."

"I don't get it," Eric said.

Jerome paused and considered what he just told us. A few seconds later he laughed. "I forgot to mention that diamonds are unique in that water *doesn't* stick to them – they can't be wetted. So when they passed the crushed kimberlite and water mixture over the beef tallow, the diamonds would stick to the grease and the rest would wash away as waste."

"What about the grease?" I asked. "How would you separate the diamonds from the grease?"

"I never actually saw them do it," Jerome admitted. "Only Dad did that. But I know he had to scrape off all the grease, heat it up in big pots, and pour it through filters. Whatever was left in the filters were supposed to be diamonds. It's actually a pretty simple mining process that's still used today."

"And only the major was involved in that final step?" Eric asked. "Your dad didn't even trust the quartermaster – his accomplice?"

Jerome shrugged. "I guess not."

"Hmm," I said. "I guess that explains how Greg and Vincent know about the diamonds. Their grandfather, Red Stevenson, must have told them stories."

Jerome nodded. "They even look like him, you know." The poor old guy suddenly looked exhausted. "Red wasn't very nice to me when the base was operating. All the other officers, pilots, and mechanics acknowledged that I was a Boy, but not Red. To be mean, he pretended I wasn't a Boy."

Eric and I looked at each other. "So he pretended you were a girl?" Eric finally asked.

"Huh?" Jerome shook his head. "What? No! A *Boy* is officially the lowest rank in the RCAF. I was only twelve at the time, but I was proud of that title. And Mickey and I had an important role – keeping the base free of rats and mice. Those were great times."

I looked at Eric again. *Yup, I think it was time for Jerome to have an afternoon nap.*

For another two hours Eric and I took turns

feeding Pluto marshmallows and making sure he made a lot of noise. I was worried the bear would tire of our antics or get sick of sugar, but he didn't. He fell into the rhythm of relaxing, scratching the walls, and eating marshmallows. I wasn't sure what Greg and Vincent were up to, but I bet they were pleased they'd found the diamonds *and* gotten rid of Jerome – without having to drown him. I'm sure they thought it was a bonus that a black bear did their dirty work and killed him. All they had to do now was wait out Pluto, which is sort of the opposite of what we were doing. We were *outside* and hoping the bear *wouldn't* leave.

Only he did leave. It happened at six o'clock when I got up to give him another chewy marsh-mallow. I placed it on the doorknob above his head and waited. But he didn't eat it. In fact, he didn't even look at it.

Jerome saw what was happening and came over and began rubbing Pluto's chin and scratching his long back. But the bear didn't feel like playing. He pushed Jerome away effortlessly and stood on all four legs. He blinked at us several times and wandered off toward the waterfront.

We were on our own.

CHAPTER 12

"**M**aybe he's just thirsty," Eric whispered in my ear. "Or going for a swim to cool off."

"Either that, or he's going into the forest to puke," I said. "I know I would."

Jerome pulled us away from the front door. "Pluto's not coming back, boys. See if you can find something to scratch the door – be quick about it. I'll stick around and delay them with bear noises."

Eric and I took off searching the camp for sound effect props that might sound bear-ish. We lucked out almost immediately when we ducked into a shed. The tines of a rusty pitchfork lay on the ground. The handle was snapped off, but we didn't need that anyway. When we got back to the quartermaster's office, we found Jerome bumping against the door and making some decent Pluto noises.

Eric held out the pitchfork and Jerome smiled.

He grabbed the short, broken handle and gave the door a good scratch – all the way from the top to the bottom. It sounded authentic from the outside, but who knew if it would fool Greg and Vincent?

Ten minutes later we heard a lot of murmuring from inside the office. Then suddenly, "HEY, BEAR, ARE YOU STILL THERE?"

"Gosh, they're dumb," Eric whispered. "Do they really expect Pluto to answer?"

"Maybe they're on to us," I said quietly. "It could be they're testing our reaction."

Jerome grunted as loudly as he could and then scratched the door aggressively. That shut them up.

After another fifteen minutes we heard the men inside talking again. The three of us listened in horror as desks and furniture were suddenly dragged away from the door.

Eric grabbed Jerome's wrist and pulled him back. "That does it," Eric said. "It's time we make a run for it."

The old guy nodded weakly.

I turned to Eric. "Take Jerome and go hide somewhere – maybe in that generator building next to the fuel tanks. I'll see if I can stall them."

Eric helped Jerome leave for the north – and safety. I knew that the old guy was doing his best, but he wasn't moving any faster than a walking pace. *Yikes!* They'd never make it away from the base in time at that rate.

I grunted as loud as I could and picked up the pitchfork tines. I scratched the door and the window, while snorting as Pluto-ishly as I could. The sound of furniture dragging on the floor stopped immediately and I grinned. *Fooled them again*, I thought.

And then I did a bad thing – a *really* bad thing.

For good measure, I decided to give the door a

final scrape near the very top. I figured that would show them just how big the bear was when he stood up. But the pitchfork got stuck in the gap between the door and the doorframe. The stubby handle popped out of my sweaty palm and fell to the ground in slow motion. That wouldn't have been a problem had the steel pitchfork landed on the soft earth. But it fell against a hard outcrop of granite and made a loud metallic *TING*. To me, the sound was deafening. And to make matters worse, the pitchfork continued to vibrate and hum like a giant tuning fork.

It was like a signal to the men inside that they were being tricked. They began yelling and shoving furniture around furiously.

I glanced north and saw Jerome and Eric still struggling to get away. Jerome looked like he was actually moving slower than when he left a few minutes earlier.

They needed more time.

I scrambled for the pitchfork and jammed it into the space between the door and the decking. Since the door opened outwards, the pitchfork would keep it closed. I picked up a rock and bashed the tines in deeper. I took a step back just as they tried to open the door.

THUMP! THUMP!

They shoved and pushed against the pitchfork. They couldn't see me, but Big Greg started yelling anyway. "You better start running, kid ... or old man ...

or whoever's out there. Because when we open this door you're dead – hear me ... DEAD!"

Eric and Jerome were finally near the forest. I sighed. They'd be out of sight in a second and I could run and meet them at the generator building.

And then the pitchfork began bending.

With each powerful shoulder bump the old metal was tiring and flexing outwards. Soon they'd be free. I turned to run ... but I didn't need to.

From the north I saw the welcoming sight of several ATVs throttling toward me. As soon as the first machine arrived at the base, I waved it over. The off-road vehicles kept coming – first two, then three, then four. By the time everyone arrived and surrounded the quartermaster's office, six quads were parked outside.

The men in the office stopped bashing the door. They must have heard the ATVs. Maybe they thought if they kept quiet everyone would just go away. I looked down at the pitchfork. All it needed was another tiny bump and it would have snapped in half – they would have been free.

A male and a female RCMP officer were driving the two lead machines. Following them were two natural resource officers and two park patrol officers. Rachel and Kelly sat as passengers behind the park patrols, and Eric and Jerome sat behind the resource officers.

The cops jumped off their vehicles before they

even rolled to a stop, and then ran over to me. They didn't ask me what I was up to because Rachel and Kelly had already filled them in. The male cop got to me first, followed closely by Eric. "Where are they?" the cop asked.

I pointed at the quartermaster's office.

The cop – his name tag said *M. Boychuk* – frowned at us. "Why are they in there?"

"They thought we were bears," Eric said.

The officer looked at the building and then back at us and then at Jerome still sitting on the ATV. "But ... but I thought they kidnapped him?" He sounded confused and I didn't blame him.

"They were going to kill Jerome ... Mr. Whiting," I said, "so we rescued him."

"I see," said the officer, though he probably didn't see anything.

"And then we trapped them in the office," Eric said, "and waited for you guys."

The RCMP officer shook his head. "Do they have any weapons that you know of?"

We told him we didn't think so and he looked relieved.

The two natural resource officers stood back with their shotguns ready, while the RCMP approached the door. The park patrol officers waited with the rest of us near the adjacent building.

Officer Boychuk snapped off the pitchfork, rapped loudly on the door, and said, "This is the

RCMP. Come on out. It's all over." He took three paces away from the door and waited with one hand on top of his handgun. I guess he wasn't taking any chances.

"Is there a bear around?" Vincent asked sheepishly from the inside. He wanted to be certain he wasn't going to be eaten, I guess.

Officer Boychuk looked at us and smiled. "There is no bear, just a bunch of law enforcement officers who want you to come out – NOW!"

The door slowly opened and Greg and Vincent came out. They glanced around, squinting and trying to force their eyes to adjust to the brightness outside. When they finally focused on the scene around them, they looked like they were going to be sick. They didn't see a bear or any blood, only three thirteen-year-olds, an old man, Kelly, and lots of angry law enforcement officers.

The cops quickly clicked handcuffs on their wrists. Greg looked up and saw me standing next to Eric. He glared at me with malice and said, "You're those kids from the gas station."

"Yeah," I said, "that's us – the *kids*."

"But ..." Greg muttered. "How did you ...?"

"None of this would have happened," Eric said, "if you had just done some basic research first, to make sure your story was believable."

Greg snarled and took a threatening step toward Eric. But the cops were ready and they held him back. "What are you talking about?"

"You told us you were diving for *Harriers*," I said. "But they never flew jets at Impact Lake. You should have told us you were searching for *Sharks*. That would have made sense."

His hand brushed against the front pocket of his jeans and he began to smirk. "Finders keepers, kid," he whispered. "That's a law that makes sense."

"Sure, that's fair," Eric said. "You found a bundle of crushed glass and you can keep it. Those sparkly little bits will look nice on the shelf in your prison cell."

"What ...?" Greg's eye's threatened to pop right out of his head.

"Or," I suggested, "you could bring them with you when you have arts and crafts class at the jail. You can write your name with some white glue and then sprinkle the crushed glass on the glue. That would make a terrific sign for outside your cell."

"And it'll remind everyone how you got duped into thinking a sack full of smashed glass was a bundle of diamonds," Eric added.

The cops holding Greg began to laugh. Officer Boychuk fished the fake diamonds from his prisoner's pocket and opened the pouch. "Wow!" he said, looking at Eric and me. "And these are all fake?"

"Yeah," I said, "They're just bits of glass from the old dump – it's over there." I pointed to the dump, but no one seemed to care where it was. Everyone was still staring at the glass in the cop's open hand – I think they thought the phony diamonds were real too.

"That was amazing timing, Rachel," I said.

"Yeah, no kidding," Eric said. "How'd you guys get everyone to believe you so quickly?"

Kelly and Rachel looked at each other and laughed. The four of us were returning to Sultana in Kelly's van, with our bikes and backpacks in the back. The police said it was okay for us to travel with her, as long as we promised to be at the police station first thing in the morning to give our statements. Greg and Vincent were on their way to a jail in Winnipeg in two separate police cars.

"We had a lot of luck on our side," Kelly said. "When we got close to town I called ahead on my cell phone. The police said that they had people in the area about to conduct a joint patrol for poachers with other officers. All we had to do was wait for them at the gas station and then guide them to the base."

"It was perfect," Rachel said, "because they already had their ATVs loaded on trailers and ready to go. I think they were excited to help – especially because of Jerome."

"What do you mean?" Eric asked.

"Well," Rachel said, "we found out that the natural resource officers have known for years that

Jerome was living at Impact Lake during the summers. They visit him once a month on their patrols in the area and they all like him. They got really upset when they heard someone was trying to kidnap and threaten him."

"But what about all those 'mad trapper' rumors?" I asked.

Kelly nodded, but kept her eyes on the highway ahead. "Apparently, it was the natural resource officers who started those rumors and kept them alive for so many years."

"Why?" Eric said. "Why would they do that?"

"They took comfort knowing he was there – over near the base – because he acted as an unofficial caretaker. He trapped the mice and –"

"So someone was paying him to catch mice?" I said.

Kelly laughed. "I asked the same question, Cody. No. He just took it upon himself to continue to keep the base free of rodents. During the war, when the base was full of people and delivery trucks came and went, they had a real pest problem. But that stopped as soon as the base closed and he doesn't catch many mice now. I guess he figured since he was watching over the base anyway, he may as well do something to keep it orderly. Like I said, he was an *unofficial* caretaker and the military had no idea he was living on the site –"

This time Eric interrupted. "How do you know that?"

"I looked into that before I came out here. I wanted to know if I'd have any contacts at the base to show me around. But there was no record of any long-term security or maintenance personnel employed at Impact Lake. The Air Force put up the KEEP OUT signs at the end of the war and then probably closed the file on the base."

Eric and I nodded.

"Anyway," Kelly said, "Jerome kept an eye on the place and the mad trapper rumors discouraged visitors and vandals from shooting up the buildings or burning the place down. So in exchange, the local natural resource officers let him live in the underground bunker for the summer. He was like their on-site deputy ranger."

"I wonder what will happen to him now," I said.

"Once the doctors have examined him at the hospital, the police will interview him," Kelly said. "But after that, I suppose he's free to go back to Impact Lake."

We had already filled in Kelly and Rachel with all the small details of our fake diamond ploy and hostage recovery operation. They both stared at us in disbelief when we told them how we used Pluto to separate Jerome from the kidnappers and then to trap them in the office. Kelly kept shaking her head, while Rachel smiled at me.

"I kind of feel sorry for Jerome," Rachel said. "Not just because of today, but also because he spent all those years searching for some stupid diamonds – diamonds that might not even exist."

"But at least he knows that now," I said. "He told Eric and me that he regrets all those wasted summers. Now he stays at Impact Lake because he likes it, not because of diamonds."

When we got to Sultana, Kelly dropped us off with our bikes at our houses. First she went to Eric and Rachel's. As Rachel got out of the van, Kelly gave her a business card. "Before I forget," she said, "here's my contact information. I hope we can stay in touch after this is all over. You kids saved Mr. Whiting and I think you may have saved me too."

"It would be great to work with you again some time," Rachel said, eagerly taking the card. "See you tomorrow at the police station."

Then Kelly drove to my place and let me out.

"Thanks for the lift," I said.

"No problem," she closed the sliding rear door and turned to face me. "By the way, I'm going to make a strong recommendation that the base be turned into a National Historic Site. There's just way too much history there for it to be forgotten."

"That's good," I said. "Except … poor Jerome."

"Why do you say that?"

"How's he going to feel about the base – his base – suddenly becoming a tourist attraction?"

"He's ecstatic," Kelly said.

"Huh?"

"You kids knew that he didn't want people to go to the base, right?"

I nodded.

"Well, that wasn't because he was a stickler for military rules, or privacy, or anything like that. It was because he wanted to preserve the base. He felt it was his job to protect the site from fire and vandals, until it could one day become a Historic Site. His dream has finally come true, Cody."

"Wow," I said. "That really is terrific ... but ..."

Kelly laughed. "All right, what else is on your mind?"

"I'm glad the base won't be forgotten," I said, "and that it'll be preserved. But we can't forget about Pluto either. He might not like seeing thousands of tourists each summer."

Kelly grinned and snapped her fingers. "I knew there was something Rachel and I forgot to tell you boys."

"Huh?"

"Rachel had the same concerns you have about Pluto. So we asked the natural resource officers if there was something they could do for him – and there is. They're going to take him to the brand new Whiteshell Bear Refuge."

"What's that?" I asked.

"It's a giant, four-thousand acre preserve, set aside especially for bears. There's no hunting allowed, and all the young, old, or injured bears receive special attention – like free food, I suppose. He'll love it there. The resource officers are already making arrangements for Pluto to be transferred."

"That's perfect," I said. "It sounds like the kind of place he'd love." I imagined Pluto eating apples – maybe even marshmallows – under a shady tree with his bear pals. I smiled. *Yup, he'd be happy there.*

"Anyway," Kelly said, "if the base is turned into a Historic Site, I think I'll ask to manage it." She gave me a wink and hopped in behind the wheel. "And if I manage the site, I'll be pretty busy. So I'll probably have to hire three smart assistants to help me."

I stayed at the curb and watched Kelly drive toward the motel where the police had booked a room for her. After years of gossip and rumors, the training base was finally going to become an official National Historic Site. I had to wonder if our involvement had any bearing on Kelly's decision. Probably not, but on the other hand, maybe we helped guide her in the right direction.

I smiled and went inside.

Mom and Dad weren't home but there was a small sticky note stuck on a larger piece of paper on the kitchen counter. I read the small message in Mom's handwriting:

Hi Cody, We're at the restaurant. See you later. Mom.

P.S. This e-mail came today. Thought I'd print it and save you the trouble. Looks interesting.

I unfolded the larger paper and began to read the

e-mail. My family had a shared e-mail account and Mom sometimes printed out the stuff that came for me. The e-mail I was reading now was from Anna, and it was making my hand shake like mad. After the third line, I had to hold the message steady with my other hand in order to finish it.

Oh my gosh!

I stuffed the paper in my pocket, ran from the house, and hopped on my bike. Five minutes later I was at Eric and Rachel's place. I saw them both sitting at the kitchen table when I got to the steps. I walked right in without bothering to knock. My face must have given something away.

"What's wrong, Cody?" Rachel said.

"We got another e-mail today from Anna." I pulled out the paper and passed it to Rachel. She was closer to me than Eric was. "Mom printed it and left it for me in the kitchen."

Rachel began reading.

"So what does it say?" Eric asked.

I ignored Eric and waited for Rachel to finish.

"Jeez, you guys," Eric said, frustrated. "Can someone please read it out loud or tell me what it says."

Rachel took a deep breath and looked up. "Guys, I think I know what we're doing for the rest of our summer ..."

About the Author

Andreas Oertel was born in Germany and has spent most of his life in Manitoba, Canada. Fascinated by archaeology, ancient civilizations, and discovery, he can often be found exploring the local beaches with his trusty metal detector. In addition to creating "**The Archaeolojesters**" series, Andreas is also the author of the young adult novel *Deep Trouble* (Write Words Inc., 2008). He lives in Lac du Bonnet, Manitoba.

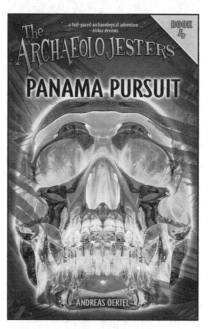

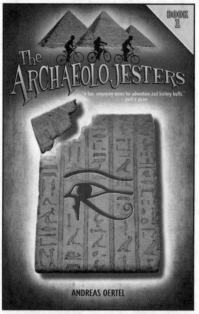

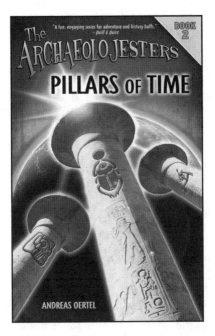

The Archaeolojesters, BOOK **2**
PILLARS OF TIME

978-1-897550-92-2

Cody, Eric, and Rachel thought they were traveling to Egypt to tour
the ancient ruins, but instead find themselves on a rescue mission in
a world beyond their imagination. Will their quick thinking and
knack for history be enough to get them home?